one hundred onehundredworders...

book Four of the Short Stories collections

Yossi Faybish

Yossi Faybish

Original title
one hundred onehundredworders...
book Four of the Short Stories collections

Editor
Yossi Faybish

Layout and Publishing
Aquillrelle.com

ISBN 978-1-4478-2786-3

I have great faith in fools; self-confidence my friends call it.

Edgar Allan Poe

Table of contents

one hundred onehundredworders...

Dear Diary...

I woke up two minutes ago. The sirens' wail this time so different from the sound of my alarm clock... I rush to my computer... this is my first entry for today. It is 5:22am... so early... My father pulls a chair across from me and sits watching me strangely. My mother sits on the floor at his feet, her head on his knees, crying, her whole body shaking. I feel Rex's muzzle against my leg, looking for consolation, he always hated loud noises...

I see the streak across the skies... a mushroom...

*

museum exhibit 312, year - approximately 2054ac

Behind The Door...

The door wasn't locked. I entered quietly and approached the bed. She lay there sleeping, my wife, my reason for being, the one I loved beyond life, beyond pain. Smiling angelically in her sleep, her lips partly open, her naked white skin soft, slightly glowing. I smiled as I remembered the poem I wrote her yesterday, the refrain painting vibrant colors in my mind:

your white of breast
against my chest...

Her white breast now cupped in his tanned hand. I took out the revolver from my pocket, pulled back the hammer... I don't remember the bullet cracking my skull...

Red On White...

I heard the tire exploding, left front. The steering wheel tore out of my hold and all I could do was watch the concrete pillar rushing towards me...

I heard voices, hardly penetrating through the bandages hugging my head. My wife's broken, sobbing. The other authoritative, soft.

"...from the neck down, irreversible. Some movement left in his left hand."

The door clicked shut, no one aware I woke up ten minutes ago. My left fingers moved slowly, hooking into the thin tube, pulling sharply. I watched fascinated the red fluid slowly crawling into a crack on the polished white floor...

Profession...

I am a sentimental slob, and one day this is going to cost me dearly. I know, I simply know. And this time now, once more, I allowed sentiment take control over my better judgment when I entered the little church and watched the beaming couple standing side by side.

So I waited patiently for the ceremony to end.

"I do", said she. Smiling.

"I do", said he. Beaming.

They kissed. Then I shot them both through the heart. I don't believe in unnecessary cruelty.

I did not shoot the priest, of course. They did not pay me for this.

The Lab...

If I knew then what I know now I would have grown bananas. I don't remember if it was in my *"To Do"*'s, have to check my lab notes. Pretty sure I had it already designed by the time. Why bananas? Firstly - it is yellow, blehhh... Secondly - one has to peel before one bites, allows them reflection time, you know...

I took my telescope and looked down again. Oh, my Me, what a mess... Guess it's time for a new cleanup. Pity, so much time lost. Let's see, what will I call him this time?

Definitely NOT Adam...

Life...

He was huge, drunk. He pushed her to a corner and hit her. Then again, and again. Then he raped her.

Wailing sirens, white corridors, white coats, the raised scythe hesitating in the black hooded creature's hand...

*

Three months.

"Now you know. You decide." White coated personnel. Impassive.

She looked at them, barely alive. The blue stains on her skin competing in beauty with the green of her eyes. The growling tiger waking inside her wounds. No hesitation.

"Life", she said.

*

Scream. Delivery. Deliverance. A little black curly head suckling love from a soft pale white breast. Life, she said.

Trex

I don't remember falling asleep last night. I woke up to sounds of screaming and running feet, people dispersing in all directions, cars honking... Suddenly I felt frightened, lost, I should have listened to her... *Mom*... I yelled and started running aimlessly like everybody else, just to get away from here, anywhere. I stopped, hesitating. Why was this man pointing a tube at me?... I saw a flash, a thunder, the pain in my eye terrible... as I was collapsing the last sounds I could hear was a strident laughter and... *damn dino*...

Mom... my tail threshed one last time.

Verdict

"You should appeal," my lawyer screamed, "you will win, the jury was split."

Of course it was split, I did not do it, it was all circumstantial. But I will not, she has a life, I have none.

I entered the glass cage, chains clinking, the red sleeve going up, the first needle going in. I looked up at the witnesses' window, she was there with her husband, crisp, crying.

"I love you" I formed the words with my mouth, everybody thinking it was for my mom. I smiled satisfied, watching the plunger drive the yellowish liquid into my vein.

Oh, So Beautiful

I looked at her as she approached me, invisible to all but me, a big smile on her face, a rose in her left hand, her right fist closed, tight. She approached, slid the rose in my shirt's pocket and pushed against me kissing wildly. I felt the sting of a thorn piercing my chest, and as she let go I saw the growing red stain on my shirt. She opened her fist...

"...this is my dream..." ...and golden dust flew into my wound.

I gasped...

"...you gave me your eternity..."

She smiled...

"...for your mortal love..."

Oh, so beautiful...

The Incredible Journey

I arrived home, crying.

"Pregnant..." I wailed.

OK, after everybody finished laughing, about three days later, I showed them the ultrasound. My father started screaming "I'll kill the bastard..." *(sorry papa...)*, my spouse "I'll gouge their eyes out..." *(careful there...)*, my mother "get the doctor now..." *(he hanged himself...)*, my dog "woof..." *(thanks buddy...)*.

Finally everybody calmed enough to hear that it was not adultery, the incredible egg journey, the womb anomaly...

Seven months later I delivered by C-section a sweet red headed baby girl...

Oh, I forgot to present myself... John my name.

Of course bottle feeding, what else?

Thrice One Hundred Words Of Love

"Do you know that every second the sun loses billion billions of kilograms of matter into energy?" I asked her, trying to sound knowledgeable.

"I know," she said, nonplusing me. *"And it all ends up with me,"* she added, opening her shirt, tearing away her brassiere and placing my palm over her breast. My mouth found hers with no additional help, moments before the flare escaping with her breath crawled its gigawatts of energy into my lungs crashing head-on with the one crawling through my fingertips, turning my insides into a blazing inferno. *"By the way, what is a kilogram?..."*

*

I rang her up... had to, mental... A sleepy voice answered.

"Hello..."

"Sorry, love, I know you are asleep, sorry to wake you up, have to tell you..."

"It's fine..." yawn... *"...don't worry..."*

"Oh, so sorry, really..."

"That's OK, wait, let me prop myself up..."

"Are you sure?... I feel so bad..."

"Stop making a fuss... I'm fully awake now..."

"Fully?..."

"If I say so..."

"Thank God, I was afraid you'll be upset, have to tell you..."

Giggle.

"So tell, finally..."

Beep... Damn!... my battery ran out. Damn!... did she know what I wanted to say?

I hope she did...

*

We picked at the bowl of nuts, talking, smiling. One hand holding, one hand blindly picking a nut. We knew it was the last one when our fingers met over it.

"You take it."

"No, you take it."

"We split it, OK?"

I popped it my mouth and cracked it.

"Wait... what about my part?..." she yelled, stabbing a finger into my mouth. I almost bit it off, then carefully guided it inside my mouth and let her pull it out.

You should have seen the smile on her face when she saw the round piece of metal around it...

Thrice One Hundred Words Of Love, Two

"Will you ever leave me?..." she wrote with blue ink on the sheet she handed me.

I took the paper, adding several wriggles till all the text was connected, blew over slightly to dry it, then with infinite patience I started scrapping the ink off. Finally a one molecule thick complete text was lying on the table.

She watched incredulously as next I took the sheet of paper, split it thickness wise in two, and placed these next to the text.

"Nobody can do it..." she said, "...it is impossible."

"Nobody loves you as much," I answered." It is impossible."

*

She was heavy, getting heavier the nearer we got to the bed. I lay her down and the mattress sank to the floor till it was cigarette paper thin.

"What is that?" I asked, frightened.

She took my palm and whispered into it, closed my fingers over the whisper and the mattress popped up like shot from hell.

"What is that?" I asked again, still uncomprehending.

"Listen to it," she said.

I brought my fist to the ear and opened it slowly.

"*Love...*" I heard the whisper dissipating into the room, and my feet started sinking into the concrete floor.

*

The dry laundry piled up in a basket next to her feet, three feet high. She just finished folding the t-shirts, pants, now she was busy folding underwear.

"You fold your underwear?"

"I fold anything I like." I did not like that look in her eyes. "Lie down," she commanded. I obeyed.

Her hands started folding me expertly – my ankles, my knees, my waist, chest, neck, then she smoothed the folding creases, kissed my flattened mouth and dropped me in her shirt's pocket. Against her breast. Against her heart.

"And also some things I love..."

Oh, the softness, the music...

Thrice One Hundred Words Of Love, Three

"All evil words start with a *D*," I declared pompously. *"Destruction, Darkness, Disappointment..."*

"Dear, Darling..." she chipped in.

"Yes?..." I answered absent mindedly and continued my barrage... *"Despair, Doom..."* before her words sunk in and I skidded to an embarrassed halt.

"Daisy, Dahlia, Daffodil..." she added, smiling.

"Even in other languages," I tried to insist, "in Romanian, *Drac* is satan."

"In Romanian, *Dragoste* is love," she added suavely.

"Death..." I tried feebly.

"Devotion, Democracy, Delicious..."

It was a losing trail, I had to stop my rampant *Dementia* fast. I stopped, wondering... does she still love me?

"Does!..." she smiled... *Devilishly.*

*

Luckily... *luckily?...* it remembered our contract. The lamp post. I was sunk in dark thoughts till I saw it rushing towards me just yards down. Something pulled the steering wheel away. Not me. I regained control of the car, watching the diminishing yellow light blinking behind, a short-circuit?... short-long-short-short, pause, long-long-long, pause, short-short-short-long... I started getting it. Does not matter it remained off afterwards, after all you cannot expect a lamp post to spell correctly.

The car-phone rang.

"Short..." was all she said.

Women, always taking the easy way out. I fell in love, madly. Life was never more beautiful.

*

"All I have is one hundred words" I told her across the table.

"This is all which is needed," she answered, taking control of my hand, "if they are the right words."

I prayed they were, and started voicing them.

"Love, love, love..."

"Wait, this is cheating," she chimed. Were these disappointment tears in her green?

"Love, love, love..." I continued adamantly, disregarding the tears.

Finally I stopped.

"I counted only ninety nine..." tears welled like a tidal wave.

"I know. The one hundredth is... *eternal.*"

They flooded my cheeks, giving that unending kiss the surrealistic salty tinge of... eternity.

Thrice One Hundred Words Of Love, Four

or *The Lab, Three*
or *Graduation*

We were still at clay modeling stage. After living three years with humans, each was requested to design a perfected version of "his" human.

I watched my colleagues, puffing up male torsos, trimming down female waists, crude yet meaningful interpretations. I trimmed down my female's breasts, puffed up her waistline...

"What are you doing?" asked my instructor, eyebrow up.

"Creating perfection," I answered.

"You are just copying reality."

"Sometimes reality is perfect," I challenged back, knowing I failed the exams.

Well, I passed. Seems that He gave the order. I wondered why, looking at my silent piece of unformed clay.

*

The second year was a toughie. Luckily I had a she-instructor who seemed to be more understanding. Everybody else was experimenting with other improved humans, I chose to stay with mine. This time the year end assignment was with real flesh, lifeless, real. I peeked at the others, all creating variations on the Schwarzie theme, Barbie, mine looked like... *her.*

Almost complete, I was desperately looking for the final detail...

"Is this what you are looking for?" the instructor smiled, pulling a single reddish hair from her pocket. I stuck it on my human. Complete.

I passed with flying colors.

*

Third year. Final graduation. Toughest.

Lifeless Schwarzie's and Barbie's side by side and then... my mold. We lined up each in front of our creation waiting for a sign from Him. It came. Everyone placed a finger on their model's mouth, the torsos shot up for a moment, then fell lifelessly back to sounds of clapping and applause.

I waited, then bent and placed my mouth against hers. Gasps. Uproar. Disgusted shouts... *artist*... *imperfect*...

All except... Him.

"You are condemned to an eternity of memories, you know..."

"Better than an eternity of regrets," I answered, and kissed life into *wife*.

Three Hundred Birthday Wishes

"Do you know how old I am today?" you ask, lining your eyes with a purple crayon and following my moves in the mirror.

"Of course. Twelve thousand four hundred nineteen."

"Sorry?... do I look that old?"

Frown.

"Twelve thousand four hundred nineteen... days."

Smile.

"You count birthdays in days?"

"Birth-*days*, isn't it? And it gives me more occasions to celebrate."

The smile grows.

"Then you should have counted in hours."

"I actually do. Better still... I do it in minutes."

I should have said seconds. I now get a kiss every single minute... for the rest of my life.

*

You get into the game.

"And how old are you?"

Easy.

"Zero."

This puzzles you.

"Not as old as time?"

"Sorry?... do I look that old?" I smile. "No, *as old as time* is next story. Zero."

You touch my forehead with your lips, not kissing, just checking my temperature.

"You are not sick. Explain?"

"Simple, every time you kiss me it's my first breath ever, you reset my age counter to *reborn*. And since you kiss me every minute... Actually, babyhood has advantages – I can talk gibberish, drool, burp..."

You blush deep scarlet before adding...

"... suckle my breast..."

*

"Your hundred worders have always three stories. One is still missing," you say between two kisses.

"No, this is the third. And you know the answer already – *as old as time*. All you have to do is find the question and the story is complete," I interrupt my suckling to say, then return to it.

Stalemate. For a few hours we change roles then return to the original ones, better. Please understand, we don't sleep too much with all this *activity* going on.

Suddenly, around 2am you smile... *finally*... (and *about time*, I think suavely).

"How old is our love?"

One Hundred Words Of Woman

pageantry

"Let's see," said the judge, "anorexia class zero, no plastic nose or breast or butt, hmmm... liposuction?... I see, neither, just birth stretch marks..." he scratched his head. "Anything... else you may want to show to the panel?"

You showed him your scrub eroded palms, your flowers planting dirt encrusted fingernails, your shopping with the kids sun burns, sleepless red eyes, no-label gown, feminist pamphlets... You did not stand a chance.

He inspected the others, young, firm, shining, he reached his decision.

"Woman," he said, "beautiful."

You did not wear your crown, you donated it to an animal shelter organization.

*

shared

"If you insist..." she smiled, passing in front of me through the door I opened. "If you insist..." she smiled, sitting on the chair I pulled out for her and sticking in her hair the flower I bought for her outside the restaurant. "If you insist..." she winked allowing me to lead the dance, to undress her, to paint her body the colors of caress and kiss and passion...

"Don't insist..." she said as I bent to carry her suitcase. She picked it up and carried it to the car. "Some things I do myself."

So beautiful, feminine. So woman.

*

kid

We drove in silence through the sleeping streets. "I am taking you to a very special place, not far away," she said about half an hour ago, and she was still driving. "Are we there yet?" I asked one additional half hour later, enjoying the drive, curious. "Patience," she admonished, intent on avoiding the potholes. Patience I had infinite, as long as she was there...

She parked in the absolute darkness, mid of nowhere, I looked around, a bit scared... "Here?..."

"Get out of the car," she advised, out of breath. "Look up." She almost cried.

I gasped... my goodness, the billion blinking lights on the pitch blank canvas. I watched her for a moment, I swear I could see the glow in her face, the reflections in her tears, the glint in her smile.

"And you thought you could catch all this beauty in just one hundred words? Very presuming of you."

"OK, what about two hundred and an apology?"

"Apology accepted," she snuggled into me, her lips a big round O like the Orion her big round eyes were glued to. I looked up at her, my own sky.

"A kid," I thought, "a woman absolute. So beautiful."

Nothing To Do With Little Red Hood

We were in love. Married, not to each other. It was clear from the way we held hands.

"Why did you dye your hair black?" he asked me.
"I hunger for your black eyes," I answered.
"Why are your green eyes red?" he asked me.
"I thirst for your blood," I answered, licking my lips.
"Why are your teeth so sharp?" he asked me.
I could not hold back any longer, I snarled then pounced and bit, and bit...

Later.

I lighted two cigarettes, one for him...

Hey, wait a moment, what did you think?... Your imagination, my friends... oh-la-la...

Barrier

Tired... you fell asleep, mouth open, curled on your side of bed.

I started snoozing... a jab awoke me. Seems you scooted over. I moved further giving you space. Then further when your elbow hit me. Then... Finally I found myself on half a foot mattress, the rest of the bed yours, but so proud for not disturbing your sleep.

Morning. Your eyes swollen, a leg hooking over me.

"Where were you all night, wanted to cuddle and make love?..."

Well, my butt is still blue from kicking myself the rest of the day. Speaking about "language barrier" between species...

One Hundred Body (p)Art(s)

small holes

First she smiled at me. Then she tried to calm me. Then had to sit on me as I was about to tear those inch wide horse straps binding me to the chair while a female *de Sade* kept drilling her needle into my skin. "Color?" "No color!" I screamed, and my sweet redhead had no choice but to feed me her breast.

I fell asleep, sweet buzzing music lulling me...

I woke up to sights of this beautiful tattoo... "Color?" asked my redhead. "More..." I pouted my lips evocatively.

They didn't even have to strap me down this time...

*

big holes

"Just one small piercing?"

This time I did tear through the straps, crashed through the window and smashed sideways into a nuns touring bus. Three hundred fourteen bucks worth of damage, and a pending lawsuit for indecent exposure of my... what the hell?... well, it was my ear if you insist.

"Whoosey..." she hiccupped when her laughter finally ended, "...this hurts more..." and she bit my ear. Wild lovemaking followed with some real indecencies embedded.

"Hey, when the hell?..." my razor hand froze mid motion as I watched the earring dangling insolently from my ear.

She hiccups to this day.

*

dare

I kicked in the door to the GayPride bar and entered, proudly flexing a stamp size tattoo on a pale bicep and trying to look confident. The Persian rug human monsters with full body designs ranging from Disney to Dali choked on their beers, as I proudly downed a double Pepsi and started on my way back out.

Someone slapped my butt.

Nobody, but I mean NOBODY (except for *her*) slaps my butt. I broke his nose.

"Colors... finally..." she delighted smiling tenderly, and tending to the red and blue and black bruises beautifully decorating my body head to toe.

One Hundred (Thousand) 'I Love You's

but who's counting?

I reached thousand seventy *I love you*'s when she started fidgeting.

"Are you bored?" I asked. Meanwhile she finished three rounds of laundry, drove twice to Thrifty's, finished "Anna Karenina" and was getting ready to pick her nose... no, she did NOT!

"No..." she yawned, pouted *insulted* and disappeared pompously into the bathroom. After fifty minutes I fell asleep at four thousand eighteen.

I had a nightmare... someone shaking me... I woke up, she was shaking me.

"Four thousand nineteen!..." she threatened me with the shampoo. How the hell?...

"I love you..." I obliged, "I love you, I love you..."

*

life and death

"You're annoying, just like the kids' *Mom... Mom...*"

I stopped the *I love you*'s flow, stuck a mental tongue her way and continued out of *earsight*. Only the dog looked at me strangely, couldn't get out of *his earsight*. I kept thinking it while eating, making love, repeating it loudly as she fell asleep...

I fell asleep. I woke up frightened to sounds of choking. Her face blue, her mouth gasping for air... I panicked.

"I love you, I love you..." I started calling. Her breast rose, then fell... *thank God...*

Guess what I did the rest of the night...

*

smart ass

She did not keep count. I did.

"The number of times I said *I love you* is fourteen thousand three hundred fifteen."

"Wrong..." she stated nonchalantly. This pissed me for real. I picked up my piles of notes, recordings, time and hour...

"See? Irrefutable proof." She dismissed it with a lazy sigh. "Bet?" I challenged.

"Bet," she agreed. "If I win then... once more?..." I was dead, but... hell, I was a winner, I agreed. "Fourteen thousand three hundred sixteen," she smiled angelically. "You forgot the one in your statement."

Dead or not, I had to do *it* once more.

One Hundred Words Of Pain And Beauty

Fiftyish, always drinking hot chocolate at the table served by me. Always tipping nicely, never trying to hit on me. Mary, the oxygenated waitress kept needling me... *he is infatuated with you... hey, what can you lose, make a few easy bucks...* winking knowingly.

One day I pulled the chair to his table, and sat across from him. *Mister, you are wasting your time. You are a nice guy but I am married. Is your wish?...* I did not finish my sentence.

He got up, smiling, leaving the usual tip... *one day, maybe, I will tell you...*

He never returned.

*

He was drunk. I hit him and left him bleeding, dropping the note I received yesterday... *your husband lost thousand bucks... pay immediately or your kid...*

I wore my best dress, shoes, almost new nylons, paid my entrance fee... *are you crazy, woman, maximum ever auctioned was hundred...* I glared at him *...my problem, punk...*

I went on stage, whoring like human cattle, asking a start price of one thousand to sounds of drunken laughter.

Five thousand... I heard a voice, choking all laughter, all counter bids. I went over, crying. He counted them into my palm. Then... he left.

*

I divorced the garbage who fathered my kid. I worked in the same café, from time to time looking sadly at that empty table. I was surprised one day being summoned to a local lawyer, who handed me a key and a bank address. *The other key is with the bank, all fees paid. He named you as his beneficiary.*

He? Who he?

I went to the bank, intrigued, curious, opened the small safe box. There was a thick envelope, heavy with hundred dollars bills. On top, there was a note: *sorry, guess that now I will never tell you.*

The One Hundred Colors Of Life

red, the color of anger

I saw red. I was suffused by it, impregnated by it, my retinae on fire, my mind a bleeding leprechaun, my muscles taut violin wire.

It took me hours to regain my vision. Actually, I was not completely sure I wanted to.

"My goddess..."

"You mean – *my goodness*."

"I mean... I always thought red was the color of anger."

A nightingale laughed, then a nightingale sang, then... well, you know what I mean.

"Red is the color of my hair, silly," she laughed, she sang... "oh, and the color of love," she added. Then she proved it to me.

*

green funnies

I was running out of metaphors.

"...green, like stomach ache, like a caiman's belly..."

"...in a green stinking swamp, rotten weeds hanging down..." she laughed. "You're not very complimentary today, huh?" I wasn't probably listening, so she continued... "...green like the princess' countenance waking up to the toad... so it *was* a legend after all..." she squirmed, turning a laughing mess.

Finally my mind clicked in.

"Green," I said "like the grains of sand growing into these pearls hiding behind the blinking shells hiding your eyes."

She ran out of laughter, probably. Else, why did she start suddenly kissing me?

*

like white

"...like unpicked cotton bleached by intolerant suns and crawling with unidentified brown beetles..."

"Freckles..." she objected, watching me trace a pink, strangely rugged path radiating away from her nipple. "And these are milk valleys," she said, "when the milk dried out the skin kept its memory."

I traced my way back, my finger resting on the nipple.

"...like a wolf's tired trace in the freshness of snow, like irregularly nibbled holes in the whiteness of a daisy's petal... Like life."

"Like love." Well, as long as she was the color in my life, she could call it anything she wanted...

One Hundred Giggles

Click. *"Hello..."*

The voice, usually a drop of mercury on a wobbly well polished marble top, now rather a pot of honey settled and thick with fatigue and sleep.

"Shit..." I screamed in the mouthpiece, not having intended to wake you up, now waking you even more. Frustrated, I searched for a tree to bang my head against, there was none as I was in the car. I banged my head instead on the steering wheel, three times. For the rest of the day I walked around proudly wearing this huge lump on my forehead, minding not the perched pigeon.

*

My colleague looked insolently at my lump, uninterested in the poop on my shoe.

"Rhinoceros?" he snickered.

"Yes," I answered, "in mating season..." and sent a hand to my belt. He shrieked and rushed away locking himself in the toilets.

I followed him, dialed the number on my cell phone, waited patiently for the sleepy *hello* on the other side and then knocked three times on the door whispering – *I love you.*

I heard a tired giggle at the other end of the world. And the thud of inert matter hitting the floor behind the door in front of me.

*

HP has regulations for anything, inclusive decent toilet usage. I was charged with indecent use of Morse code on a flat surfaced company property. The judge looked askance at the company lawyer, who fidgeted uneasily in his chair. Then moved his attention to me.

"So you knocked three times. Long or short?"

"Short, your honor, for *S*. I wanted to whish him *Shit in peace*. He fainted too early."

The judge hit his gavel three times.

"Three long ones for *O*, *Out of here...*" Then he threw the gavel at the lawyer and fell off his chair convulsing in laughter.

The Lab, Four

or *Perfection in 100, 50, and even 25 Words*

100

It was time for the final test. I picked the prototype marked *Adamtwo* from the shelf and said,

"Love..."

It teared. I tweaked a bit the heart, listening carefully...

"...love..." I said again, and it teared again. I frowned and tweaked some more, this was not going as well as I planned.

"Love."

Nothing. Thank me. Satisfied, I returned it to the shelf and after some hesitation – I removed the *w* from its name. *Adamto*. I did not want anyone to ever suspect there was an earlier failed model. After all, I had my pride.

Then, I unleashed the fire.

*

50

Time for the final test, prototype *Adamtwo*.

"Love..."

It teared. Some tweaking...

"...love..." I said again, teared again. I tweaked some more.

"Love."

Nothing. I returned it to the shelf and removed the *w. Adamto*. Did not want anyone to suspect the earlier failed model.

Then, I unleashed the fire.

*

25

Prototype *Adamtwo*, final test.

"Love..." it teared.

Tweaked some...

"...love." Nothing.

Erased the *w. Adamto*, no witnesses to my previous failure.

Then, unleashed the fire.

One Hundred Intimate Moments

"Roll over," you said, forcing me to roll on my stomach. Then you slapped my fleshy bottom twice and lay your cheek on the smarting spot, sighing contentedly.

"Ouch... why did you do that?" I complained, indignation filling my voice.

"It was too cold."

"And now, is it warm?"

"Not really..." I heard and felt the smack of a kiss. *"But now you are branded with my mark."*

I rebelled, without actually pulling away.

"What am I, cattle?" my indignation tone rose one notch higher, but I was talking to the wall as you were already snoring softly into dreamland.

*

We sat on both sides of the table, naked, breakfasting. I was just about to dip my teaspoon into my yoghurt when you snatched it away.

"Hey, this is mine," I wailed.

You lay both yoghurts in front of you, then rose slightly and dipped your breasts into them.

"They are both yours now," you smirked mischievously. I looked questioningly at the teaspoon in my hand. *"You can do better than that,"* you goaded my intellect.

I guess I could and did. And if you don't know what I'm talking about, I guess you better not be reading this story.

*

"What color are my eyes?" you asked.

"I don't know, it's dark."

You turned on the bedside lamp.

"And now?"

I moved my head from the comfortable position between your breasts to the muscle stressing position of carrying it on my neck. The reflection blinded me.

"Looks like there is a lamp in them..."

I hated to see that big tear bubble rolling.

"Try again..."

I shifted my viewing angle till I saw my own reflection.

"Looks like I am in them."

This time you smiled, letting me return to the safety of your bosom.

Women... sometimes acting so weird.

Those Fifty Word Legends Of Love... (Retold)

of frogs?

Poor frog, hopping alongside me, competing for that kingdom frog-elders tell their children about. Doesn't it know that's a legend?

I lower it into the pond, turning around right into your kiss... mmmmm...

Damn!... I must control my reflexes, my coiled tongue almost shooting out to that fly buzzing by...

*

of kids?

"Hansel?..."

"Yes, Gretel."

"Are you sure we will find our way back?"

"Yes," I say confidently, strewing the breadcrumbs behind us.

"Hansel... the breadcrumbs are gone..."

"Don't worry, Gretel," I calm your fears, "look back," I say, pointing to the tiny daisies popping up wherever your foot left the ground.

*

of wood?

"Hey, Pinocchio!..." you smiled, blowing kisses my way.

I knew I was not supposed to fall in love, after all I was made of wood.

But then... you kissed me.

"I love you," I hardly had the time to say before the flames escaped my heart and invaded my body.

Counting One Hundred Miracles Of Love

oddly even

"Something's wrong," I said, "there are two moons."

"Yes, and this morning there were two suns," she laughed, "you should get your eyes checked. Or your brains..." she added after a smacking kiss.

"Oops, two falling stars," I started incredulously.

"Anything four of?"

"I don't know about four, but it's so odd that everything is even... two's and four's and eight's..."

She smiled knowingly and kissed me again. I guess she knew something I didn't, and now was playing coy with me.

I gave up trying to understand the miracle and finally gave up also looking into her eyes. *Hey!...*

*

oddly odd

"And now maybe *you* can explain to *me* my miracle?" She kept counting and recounting her fingers and her toes and it always came up to nineteen. Yet all the usual fingers were there when she looked for them hard enough. She wasn't a great believer in the worlds *beyond*, but the facts were so oddly odd... "Shall we call in the *missing fingers* department?..." she giggled uneasily.

I was as baffled as she was, though I could not fully concentrate on her miracle, busy as I was sucking her fingers and toes in my mouth, one after the other.

*

even odd

"Even odd numbers divide by two."

"But then the result is a fraction."

"Not necessarily. Divide one apple by two and you get two half apples, each one a complete half apple, not a fraction. An entity."

"That's philosophy, not math."

"OK, then take us, we are one pair of lovers. But divide us by two and we become two lovers."

"That would be a miracle. Divide us by two and we become nothing."

She had a point there, I hated to admit. No, not really hated, rather... loved to admit. Miracles don't exist. Math is after all a science.

One Hundred Statistical Love Declarations

statistics

I picked a fistful of pebbles and threw them up in the air, watching them fall. Some raking passing cars windshields, some exploding into the deep dust. Some landed back into my hand. I looked at them disinterestedly.

"Statistics," I said.

"Fate," you said. Then you took them from my hand and stuffed them inside your shirt's pocket.

"Why do you do that?" I asked, wondering.

"Next time you will not be able to pick these anymore."

"So?" I insisted.

"No more statistics," and seeing my rising eyebrow you smiled impishly. "Fact," you said. "Absolute," you said. "Love," you said.

*

chance

"All those trillions of missed human beings - wasted ova, wasted sperm, coincidental encounters resulting in incidental individuals growing in conjectural environments..."

"My goodness, you really know all these long words?"

"...multiplied by the probability of brain paths and intonational quality of consonants mixed with an enormous selection of vowels to create words and mix these into expressions... our chance of existing and meeting are zero," I concluded triumphantly.

"I love you."

I blinked, lost in this simplicity countering all my complexity. And had to admit once your hand reached a certain anatomical evidence that... gulp... we very much existed.

*

lottery

I pulled the first leaf, playing statistics and probabilities in my head, fearing to lose, certain to lose... and yet choosing to say...

"Loves me not," sweating my fear through constricted airways.

Whence your confidence as you dared looking for the next leaf, smiling...

"Loves me."

Clover, three leaves, the chances for... I rolled it knowing there is a third leaf...

"Loves me not," and I pulled it off.

We did not know, the odds infinitesimal, your smile unabating. We rolled it further...

"Loves me!" you shrieked your delight, pulling the fourth showing leaf and biting me to bleeding love.

Three Times One Hundred Loving Bees

package

I signed the receipt, tipped generously... poor postman, it was huge. Then dragged it into the house, there was a buzzing, no, no bomb, maybe a practical joke? There was no *from*, only *to*, my name with a smiley inside the *o*.

I dropped it in the hallway, showered (it WAS heavy...) then picked up the scissors. It was still buzzing. I cut a hole and an angry bee zoomed by me, loaded with pollen. I cut it completely... there was a letter inside: *a bed of petals, for you lover.*

I hope the poor bee made it back home.

*

bed

I woke up early, soft music enchanting my ears. The more I opened my eyes the more the music changed to buzz. Finally it WAS buzz, the bee having decided to take a nap before flying away. I opened a window and it kissed me, then flew out.

Who uses yellow lipstick, you asked, *and why is your top lip swollen?* you added jealously.

It was a bee, I answered oozing sincerity.

Yeah, you sneered, disbelieving and smearing red lipstick all over my body and biting my bottom lip, my ear, and some other very sensitive parts of my body.

*

commune

We rolled inside the bed, petals sticking shamelessly to various humid parts of our bodies, my nose being just one of them. We kept swapping humidity, then petals, then humidity... sometimes sharing, sometimes fighting insanely over those wet spots each wished conquered...

Aaaiii... you screamed out of sync with the music.

Told you, I said, watching the swarm getting comfortable on its side of bed, noisily gossiping our secret. I guess they all arrived while we were busy making OUR noises.

We buzzed, they talked, finally we reached equilibrium: they making honey, we making love. Together - making beauty. *Aaaiii...*

Three Times One Hundred Flowers

flowers
like you cover the field...

"I don't cover."
"You are flower."
"Then add a comma, after 'you'."
"I have many commas, do you want more?"
"One. For now..."

I was pissed off, my romantic train of thought broken. I was about to continue.

"...and remove the ellipsis."
"Which ellipse?"
"Not ellipse, ellipsis you dork, if you continue then there's no need for it."

Aha... you were in one of those objectionist moods.

I dropped the paper, the pen, dropped your body on the bed... I couldn't help praying that I was better with my fingers than with my pen.

*

I tried to finish my poem with my toes, my fingers still imprisoned in your mouth (other things imprisoned too) making it very difficult. I succeeded finally to add the comma, you moaned with pleasure and I was not sure it was at the comma.

Adding was easy, removing that eclipse thing was tougher - I tried spitting, hissing, licking... *let my mouth go*, I begged mentally. You were probably a retard, didn't understand a thing from my clicking sounds and just bit harder on my tongue.

I gave up, poetry could wait. I had some bargaining to do... mmm...

*

I finished the poem, not allowing the toe tickling my ear disturb me any longer. Your toe, not mine, smartass.

I started writing it inklessly on your skin with my freshly liberated finger, cowardly avoiding any additional remarks. Just finished writing 'polen'...

"...double l..." I heard you. How the hell?...

Clearly I lacked the talent.

"You're quite talented in other domains," you chirped.

So you *did* read minds, you wanton being.

There was only one way to shut your mouth. I did it. And I *did* finish my poem. But I couldn't erase that lecherously stupid grin off my face.

Story In One Hundred Butterfly Parts

gift

She offered me a box.

"It is alive," she said.

"What's alive?" I asked.

"It is tamed," she said.

"What's tamed?" I asked.

She puffed herself away, leaving only her smile behind. Then the smile faded as well.

I opened the box, turned it upside down. It floated to the floor as beautiful as only a butterfly can be, as dead as only a butterfly can be.

I tried *fetch!*, *roll!*, *play dead!*... seemed *play dead!* was the only command it obeyed. I put it back in the box, didn't want to step on it by mistake. I fell asleep.

*

morning

I woke up at pecking sounds. The butterfly was on the window, a bird trying in vain to snatch it away through the glass. The box lay torn on the floor, the butterfly as dead as ever. *Rover, fetch! Rover, roll!* Nothing. Strange and disappointing. I went to work.

I returned with evening, mad at my boss and mad at the big hole in the window pane. So the bird had its way after all. I swept the cardboard pieces and the glass shards under the carpet, and brooded myself to sleep. I dreamt of the butterfly turning dragon. Ridiculous.

*

midnight

This dream was of raining petals. My eyes were open... this was *not* a dream. The dragon hardly fitted inside my room, its butterfly wings raining.

"Hey, so finally *you* swallowed the bird?" I laughed. "Roll! Play dead!" I tried, and it refused. "Fetch!" I tried further, and it crashed out through the window. I reached the count of three when it returned, depositing her in my lap and turning butterfly on her breast, under my palm. Her smile followed on its own, settling on her mouth.

Well, I think I have no choice but to start believing in fairytales.

Fifty Times Three Suns And One Night's Love

The dinner was tasteless. Don't misunderstand me, the restaurant was great. The food and wine were great. Your body sublime in your sublime dress undulating sublimely on the dance floor...

Probably this was the problem. I realized everything else was perfectly tasteless once I tasted your lips. Oh, the taste...

*

The bed refused us, scared. We made love on the floor, the tiles minding not melting into their species origins' memories of furnace and molding flames, our bodies following in the turmoil and ransack of flesh.

We rested in a pothole, sleeping, smoke lifting away from cinders and smoldering skin.

*

The sun was pulling itself up by trillion trillions of tiny tendrils, all I could do was cut the millions few invading the room. I closed the shutters, closed the drapes, closed your eyes...

"In vain," you said, kissing my hand away and leaving your body's perfume in the room.

Three One Hundred Strange...

...colors

"I wonder
how would you look in cochineal panties
with viridescent fringes
and phthalo blue polka dots down the front and up the other side?"

huh?

"I try to imagine your gamboge brassiere
hanging to your nipples with matching annatto lace
and unmatching quinacridone clasps."

gulp!

I locked the doors and the windows and plugged the sink's drain, afraid you would escape, screaming.

"All I see is your white skin
your red lips
your blue eyes."

ooh...

I let go. It was tough making love holding your struggling figure down in a double Nelson. There was no need anymore, anyhow.

*

..foods

I unfolded the airtight packaging under your watchful eyes, the natural flavors imprisoned until that last fold...

oh, God... you paled, squealed, and pinched your nose turning gradually green. You refused to taste my durian, not vomiting though. I delectated in it alone, thank you.

Tried the next – some petai beans... *blahhh*... then some poi... *no, but no thanks*... then you serially refused my ambuyat, poutine, even the gingko seeds (sorry, forgot them in their fruit's flesh and almost vomited myself).

"So what other delicacy can I offer you, my love?" I asked.

Well, you undressed me and showed me.

*

...animals

I didn't want to tell you about sengis' nose, about jerboa's ears, not even about tarsier's eyes or fingers or tail.

"As a kid, I liked playing pussy..." I said, and under your scrutiny I added hastily "...liked them big. Oh, no," I smiled knowingly, winking, "not the meow kind." Why the hell did you hit me with your spiked heel? All kids liked playing tipcat.

tipcat?...

...and you couldn't stop apologizing about your behavior all the way into undressing me and making love to me. It wasn't until later that you told me what *you* meant by it. Ooh...

Erotica In Fifty Words? C'mon...

trick

"I will show you a trick," I said, placing the wine glass between her knees.

"I will as well," she replied, opening her knees, letting it fall. She kept opening until they were a sideways laid bottle apart. More.

I had to admit her trick's superiority. And her wine's too.

*

fruit

First I thought they were cherries, hanging there for me to pick. I knew they were not when she screamed... "... hey, that's my nipples."

I knew there was revenge in the air, yet I never saw it coming.

"I thought that's a banana," she grinned maliciously, as I screamed.

*

hunger

I dropped two apples in and wore her bra. She dropped an apple in and wore my shorts.

"You look appetizing," I said.

"You look delicious," she replied.

We were famished, we attacked each other's fruits ravenously.

No, no, think, the other way around... yep, the apples were for later.

Xscopy In One Hundred Stars

Eureka

I tried telescope. Then magnifying glass, finally deciding an optical microscope might be best suited. I would've tried an electronic microscope if there was a way to slice you as thin as needed.

"What are you looking for, lover?"

"Magic," I answered, carrying the microscope over your skin in steps one molecule long. You let me do, enjoying the stupidity and the tickle.

"I think it is time for other tools," you finally snickered, smashing my microscope and taking over the guidance of my fingers around your molecules... oh, that's what you meant?

"*Eureka*," I gurgled happily, before drowning.

*

Eppur si muove

I certainly didn't want to end like Bruno. Not even like Galileo. Thus I decided to keep my findings secret, though my telescope never deserted you. I mapped your mountains, your valleys, you weren't even aware... hey, a star is not supposed to be aware of scientific research.

I got a blue eye when you, nevertheless, got fed up with stardom and pushed the telescope away, going through my notes. Oh, no, will it now be the dungeon or the fire?

"Both," you hissed, rolling and rolling underneath me.

"Eppur si muove," I gurgled happily, my fire invading your dungeon.

*

Cogito, ergo sum

I decided to give up all the scopes - micro, macro, tele, kaleido... the works. It was time for me to prove I possessed also some intellectual virtues. I pointed to my head.

"Cogito, ergo sum."

You looked at me askew, licking your lips with an undeniable smirk.

"I believe there's a spelling mistake." And as I squinted quizzically, you added "You have one 'g' too many".

It did not penetrate right away. Once it did, I dropped all intellectual virtues gurgling my way happily into impending *noésis noéseós*. "Huh?..." you grunted, proving my intellectual superiority. Not that it mattered.

Irrelevant... a 55er

"Look, mom!" she pointed upwards to a moon suddenly splitting, drifting slowly apart.

I rushed to the TV, a livid presenter was being whispered something in her ear. As if keeping up appearances mattered.

I gathered the girls, the dog, rang my husband knowing there was no time for him to reach home. I waited.

Barter... a 55er

I offered her a flower. She offered me her heart. I offered her my body. She ran away.

I found her thirty-one years later.

"Do you still have my flower?" I asked.

"Do you still have my heart?"

We bartered flower against heart.

"Now I know you love me," she said, offering me her life.

Of Love, Blasphemy, And Punctuation In 25 Words

love

"So much lipstick on pillows, bed-sheets... made love to the bedding?" I asked.

She took a towel, wiping my mouth, eyes, fingertips... so much red...

*

blasphemy

Eve didn't know Adam's medical antecedents. She gave him an apple and he choked. So how'd I get to be and write this?

Hmmm... Snake?

*

punctuation

"I love you."

"*I love you!* or *I love you?*"

I thought for three days.

"You. Love! Me?"

She smiled for seven.

"I! Love!! You!!!"

The Bad-Speller's Guide To Lovemaking

w-w-w-w

"You're a lousy speller," she stated, sad. It was inexcusable for a poet to be a bad speller, I knew. "Spell love," she challenged me.

"w-i-n-e?..." I tried, doubtful, hating that big tear rolling down her cheek. She picked up her handbag.

"Try again," she gave me one last chance.

"r-o-s-e?..." I tried again, uncertain. She grabbed the door handle, turning it. "y-o-u!..." I shouted after her, desperately.

My, my, was she heavy, hanging there to my neck kissing and sobbing.

"You *are* definitely a poet," she said, "you are crazy."

"Crazy," I echoed happily, finally on familiar ground, "l-o-v-e..."

*

s-s-s-s

"Tie my feet to the bedposts," she asked, embarrassed. I obeyed, blushing. "You forgot one s," she giggled, untying then tying the right foot to the other bedpost. "Now... your tongue... to my spot..." she whispered. She must have been crazy.

I got off and touched my tongue to the flowers pot. Smelling good, still...

"Are you s-deaf or what?" she screamed, "I want my wild sex, now!"

This really pissed me off. I gave her all I had, finishing in a hurricane of appreciative grunts. She fell asleep, smiling.

I guess she'll never want her wild ex again. Ever.

*

u-u-u-u

We became friends on the net. Then lovers. Now meeting for the first time, my poem written on paper, ready to be recited to her. You see, I wasn't so sure of my accent.

I unfolded the paper and started reading.

"*The beautiful can't...*" the slap was less painful than that look of hurt.

"And I thought you were different..." she crumpled the paper.

"But I just wanted to..." I tried to hold her back.

"Butajustawantata..." she mocked me, laying down the crumpled sheet and smoothing it... "...ohh..." she suddenly gasped, turning tomato-red.

My God, was she one hot kisser...

One Hundred And None Nights Of Word, Wit, And Jealousy

name

I woke up in panic, the earthquake still reverberating in the bed's frame.

"Ouch..." she wailed, holding her forehead, there where she hit it against the bunk bed.

"Oh," I said, relieved and worried at once, "I hope you didn't lose any brain cells, Sarah," and I winked, smug in my self-appraisal of wit and double joke.

She touched the egg on her forehead.

"Well, as long as I remember my name, Jack," she winced again, smiling approvingly at my care.

My God, it was worse than I thought, her name was *not* Sarah.

And who the hell was Jack?

*

names

She tossed and moaned her side of the bed, certainly dreaming of making love to someone. And certainly not to me, as I was on the bed and couldn't be in two places at once. It pissed me off.

I shook her awake.

"The truth, this time I want the truth and the names," I demanded.

She looked at me myopically, paddled bare footed to the desk and returned with the telephone book. I was rightfully outraged.

"What?..." Then she lifted the book and hit me over the head, leaving me stunned and baffled. Women and their mysterious communicating ways.

*

nameless

I pulled my stomach in and asked belligerently.

"Aha, your good lookers out there - who are they? Brad Pitt, Michael Jackson, Richard Gere?"

"Naaah, too girlie."

"Who's left? Danny DeVito?"

"Naaah, too sexy."

"Paris Hilton?"

"Too vacant."

I ruminated, foaming, almost losing control of my stomach's muscles. I decided to change strategy, acting subtle.

"Where?"

"Here."

"What?!..." I dropped under the bed, looked behind the curtains, emptied the marmalade jars... She roared with laughter, trying to distract me with making love.

"*You*, silly."

Ha-ha, lady, not with *this* genius. Then, suddenly, it hit me... *aha, the brooms closet!*

One Hundred Declarations Of For The Love Of

choice

She was beautiful, oh, so beautiful. As Delilah must have been when she gave the shears to Samson's hair. Or Bathsheba when she drove David into deadly sin. Or Esther when she asked her king husband for Haman's life.

"It's her or me," she challenged me, the fire in her eyes burning me with promise.

I had no choice but to make a decision. I drove and dropped her somewhere, don't remember where, and returned home heart broken.

"Come here," I called her at my side, and she cuddled against my ribs, her tail beating endless love into the bed.

*

return

The knock on the door, the divine hug, the tears, the mutual apologies, the mutual passion, the mutual sex (what else?).

"I love you," we said, almost at the same moment, after some terrific sex. I offered to prepare myself the breakfast that morning as the ultimate sign of eternal reconciliation. Eggs, warm milk, buttered bread, hush brownies... she watched me all the time, making ribald remarks about my lower body parts and offering unasked for advice. Surprisingly, she was as excited as I was.

Then we sat together on the floor, holding hands and watching doggie wolf everything down.

*

bite

She bit me. The dog, not the human, you dorks. Well, she had good reason when I stepped on her sleeping form's tail and she coiled up, finding her teeth deep in my ass. The she tried to lick the place clean but I decided to take no chances and get my rabies shots.

She drove me to the institute. The human, not the dog, you dorks. The female (shit) doctor took a long look at my ass, scratching her head in embarrassment.

"For which of the two bites, sir?"

Ferrari-red is snow-white compared to my cheeks at that moment.

There Weren't One Hundred Titans, Were There?

Atlas

I was drunk. I walked to the well and puked. Then I screamed, laughing insanely.

"Hey, Atlas, what would happen if I climb down there and tickle you?"

There was some rumbling back, sounding something like hurrburrlurrisos... ancient Greek, I thought, rolling with inebriated laughter. I didn't know even modern Greek, and a poor titan wouldn't understand a word of my English. I had a terrible headache, took a sleeping pill and keeled over.

I woke-up and opened the TV:

"... never before, felt world-wide, intensity 6.1 on the Richter scale..."

By Zeus, guess someone did understand English, after all.

*

Epimetheus

Thought nothing of it when my neighbor told me his wife's name. Nor when I read on his door: Epi and Pandi. Sounded lovely.

The bell rang.

"Something to eat," she smiled, handing me a bowl. I uncovered it... mmmmm... smelled deliciously. I forgot the loose tile, twisting my ankle. Got a flat tire. I was fired. My car was impounded.

I limped (damn bus) all the way to the landfill, looking for the bowl under the strained eyes of the garbage collectors. I found it and licked desperately the bottom.

"Looking for Elpis," I sniggered, before they certified me.

*

Prometheus

"It's on the tip of my tongue, the one with fire, starts with P..."

"Pythagoras?"

"No, he was a square type."

"Ptah?"

"No beard."

"Odin!"

"Odin? That's a Norse one. And starts with O."

"Close enough. And the fornicating old-goat had so many kids, one probably starts with P. Hmm... Priapus, Polydectes, Persephone?... no. Presley?"

"Ah, got it – Prometheus."

"Never heard of. What of him."

"That stupid Zeus, wanted to punish him and instead punished me. Just the thought of liver makes me throw up. Do you know what it is to eat the same portion every day, for years?"

One Hundred Pets And Words

octopus

He walked everywhere with the octopus on his face and holding his wife's hand, soft cooing sounds enveloping them.

"My pet," he kept repeating tenderly, sticking his head from time to time in a bucket of salt water. "Mediterranean," he reassured everybody. I always wondered who/what he meant.

One day I saw him alone, just he and his octopus, sipping orange juice with two straws from a big glass.

"The bitch ran away with a dog," he complained bitterly, leaving it to interpretation while the octopus formed an "o" with one tentacle. After all, they don't have thumb and forefinger.

*

unicorn

"I have a small unicorn," I boasted.

"It looks like a goat to me," she said, doubting.

"It is a bi-corned unicorn," I insisted, combing its beard. I finished milking it and patted it affectionately on the head. "Fly, my little friend, fly..." I murmured inside its hanging ear.

She turned around, disgusted, and opened the door. She hardly had time to duck as my unicorn bleated over her head, soaring into the blue.

"And this?" she pointed a shaking finger towards the toad.

"A prince."

She just went over and kissed it. Sometimes, they invite me to their castle.

*

owl

"1+1=2" I composed on the board. Buzz, the owl, hooted once for "yes", to sounds of applause. "2+1=2" I composed, and it hooted twice for "no", for a dead mouse, and for more applause.

"Blahhh," vociferated the eternally skeptic in the first row, "no intelligence, just circus tricks."

I offered him the magnetic digits and he composed "5-5=10". Buzz flew over, playing hummingbird for a few moments, then picked up the 1 and flew it over to me. The applause was deafening. Buzz hooted once, flew over the skeptic and pooped.

Now, this is what I would call superior intelligence.

A Maker's One Hundred Times Times Three Choices

or *The Lab, Five*

time

It was dark. I heard you fumbling with the watch.

"What's the time?" I asked, sleepily.

"The time before time," you answered.

"Let's make time," I mumbled. We made love. "And now?"

You fumbled with the watch again.

"Uh-huh, something's wrong with the time."

We had no choice, we had to make time again. After the third time, I started guessing that you were fooling me. Only after the ninth time I heard the rooster.

"About time," I mumbled, slapping your hand away. "Let's deal with the light tomorrow, ok?"

"We still have to make tomorrow," you answered.

Oh, no!...

*

timeless

"People have these strange ideas. If they put *less* before the *thing* it means not so much of it, if they put *less* after the *thing* it means nothing of it." I was really frustrated with people in general and linguists in particular.

"Especially since they are so inconsistent. If they put *full* before the *thing* means basically the same as after."

For once we agreed.

"I wish we could be less minded to these mindless creatures... oops, we're contaminated."

"We have no choice but to try to make corrections," you smiled wickedly.

Oh, no, me and my big mouth!...

*

time-out

I was sore, tired, restless. Those people down there incessantly bitching, biting, barking. I needed a time-out for a hundred years at least. I started closing my eyes...

"Wake up..." you nudged me impatiently, "look what we've created." I mumbled a curse involving mainly myself as I had no parents... goodness, what was this cute, tiny, tail-wagging creature chewing my finger off?

"It's a puppy bitch." I let the little critter snuggle against me, closing my eyes again.

"Ahm... there is a slight problem," you continued. "We have to make a mate for her."

Oh, no, there goes my time-out!...

The Last One Hundred Words... Maybe

or *The Lab, Six*

"Imagine a world with ice-cream at $49.99."

"Imagine a world without ice-cream."

"Imagine a world without bread."

"Imagine a world with guns..."

There was tacit understanding between us. I opened the cloud and rested my thumb on the button.

"Wait a moment." She pulled me to her magnifying glass - a rosy-cheeked baby dragging a leash dragging a wild-eared puppy dragging a huge sunflower in its teeth, a bee buzzing in and out... I couldn't do it.

I locked the cloud behind me with an unbreakable code. I wondered if I was omnipotent enough to make me forget the code.

Inter-Racial Bliss, And One Hundred Words To Achieve It

parental bliss

I'm black. And beautiful. My mama is white and beautiful. My papa is white and Jewish. I'm black. Like the bottom of a chimney on a moonless/starless/electricityless night. Like rock before Elvis. Black.

My father checked first both genealogical trees, seven generations back. Then he wanted to strangle my mother. Then he accepted her claim for sainthood, after she swore on our neighbor's head, head on his bald head, that he was the father. DNA? What DNA? Once you adopt religion you abolish science.

My neighbors are pitch black. Almost like me. Their daughter is pitch white. I always wondered...

*

our bliss

There was one sure way to find. I married her. If the children are retarded...

The son is white like the peak of the Kilimanjaro before global warming. At age one he was solving differential equations, second degree. The girl is black like painted in Coke. The liquid one. At age two she finished reading War and Peace in original Russian. Two months later translated it to Chinese.

Want something? I asked my wife one day, after sex.

Chocolate, she answered demurely and I lay my hand on her cup. She took it away and laid it on her belly.

*

kids bliss

Poor wife, no chocolate. Twins, the boy black, the girl white, six months after birth he was singing Othello and she Desdemona. Luckily it was only Act-1, otherwise I might have lost a child. They took their acting damn seriously.

I returned from the lab, the envelope unopened. We sat down, watching the kids beat each other to death. Sometimes kids are kids.

Now is the time to know, I said.

She was quiet, watching the kids, smiling. She took the envelope from my hand and put a match to its corner.

Why? she asked. Yes, damn good question. Why?

I'm A Poet! I'm A Poet! In A Hundred Words'...Triplicate

night time

I heard her fumbling with the blanket...

"Where?" I mumbled, my mouth sticky with sleep.

"To pee..."

"Come back to me?" and I jumped out of bed, wide awake, screaming... "I'm a poet, I'm a poet!"

She crawled back, quietly.

"You're quiet, like a shoe."

"Like a blue shoe," she corrected me, and I lay there, crestfallen. She was a better poet than me.

Morning.

"Rhyme me duck," she yawned.

"Luck?" I yawned back.

"You suck..." she yawned with superiority, then proceeded to say in deed what I missed to say in word. Yes, a much better poet, incomparably better.

*

day time

She was pulling up her panties.

"Aren't you pulling up your panties?" she asked, suspicious.

"Men, don't wear panties, they wear shorts," I retorted, finally superior in something even if not poetry or... the other thing.

She started pulling them down.

"What are you doing?" I asked, suspicious.

"Proving that they do."

She did. Writing poetry all over my skin. I sat up (later) to put it also to paper. Dropped a bit of glue on the panties, proudly sticking them to the paper, ready to compare poems.

"See?" I showed her mine. She showed me hers. Still better. Damn.

*

any time

I was scratching my head, lost.

"What rhymes with roof?" I asked her.

"Woof."

Yes, maybe I could use it...

"And with plow?"

"Meow."

I looked up, something on her mind?

"Chirp?"

"*Slurp.*"

Yes, something was definitely on her mind.

"Sex?"

"*Mmm...*"

This one broke the pattern, maybe I had it all wrong to start with? "Sex!" I repeated. "*Mmm...*" she repeated. "Sex!!!" I triplicated. "*Tyrannosaurus rex!!!*" she replicated.

I should have known better, almost got my head chewed off.

"*Sooo...?*" she purred, later.

"Arooo..." I tried my best, failing. But even though the rhyming wasn't perfect, the poetry was.

Alice'an Fifty Measurements Of

happiness

You sit on my knees, naked. I'm naked too, but will save you *those* disgusting details. My palm weighs your breast, lifting it repeatedly, my thumb on the nipple.

"What are you doing?" you ask.

"Trying to attribute measurable values to happiness," I answer, my mouth a study in Cheshire'ness.

*

happiness

I sit on your knees, naked. You're naked too, magnificently so. Your palm measures something... sorry, unspecifiable, my body a study in Mock-Turtle-Reeling-and-Writhing'tivity.

You're frowning.

"What are you doing?" I ask.

"Trying to attribute a measurable value to happiness, but it's impossible. The value keeps changing," you answer, squeezing again.

*

happiness

"Happiness is clustered," I declare. "For men it's clusters like one and two and thirty-two, like two and two, like one..."

"One is not a cluster."

"Well, one and countless hairs is," my countenance a study in Queen-of-Hearts'ian red.

You ponder.

"Then, for women, it's one and two. And countless."

Fifty Tastes

dinner

"Dinner?" she asked.

"Dinner?!" I answered, wondering about her short term memory, maybe even her sanity. That's how it starts, you know. We were just past the antipasto, minestrone, calzone...

"Dinner!" she insisted, pulling the hem of her skirt one inch higher.

"Dinner!!!" I almost chocked, rushing away to... dinner.

*

dessert

She was filling the cart with vegetables, meats... I trailed her, continuously mumbling my dissatisfaction...

"...and dessert, what about dessert?"

I guess she got fed up with me and stopped suddenly. I had no choice, and stumbled right into her bum.

"Dessert..." she murmured. I stopped mumbling. I blushed, instead.

*

breakfast

...and there was a variety of bread-rolls, cold cuts, eggs, freshly squeezed orange juice. Oh, also a variety of vegetables. I guess that's all. She really enjoyed it.

Sorry, you mock me? What do you mean asking "that's all?"? Told you this was breakfast. What did you expect - sex?

The Little Prince And His Fifty Dreams

desire

"...and then the little prince said – tell me about desire."

"There's nothing about desire in the story."

"On the contrary, it is only about desire."

You were making a disbelieving face, so I placed the book down. I needed both hands, to move to the practical aspects of the session.

*

passion

"What's this?" You showed me a penciled circle.

"A breast covered by a lover's hand seen through a round keyhole."

"You could have written The Little Prince..." you purred.

"I wish I could or did. Neither. Though I understand the passionate desire in it."

I, said it. You, proved it.

*

lust

"What age was the little prince?"

"Lust age."

"Hey, he was a child."

"So was I, before you arrived."

"And who arrived in his life?"

The loophole I needed.

"You." You stare. "*His* life. Antoine's. Could anyone write such masterpiece without knowing you?"

The kiss that followed was lust. Purified.

One Hundred Times The Power Of Nature...
Yeah, Sure...

gale

5:02PM. There was a terrible gust of wind, a gale, a three seconds event reported country-wide. Luckily so short lived, otherwise...

Several trees were uprooted, a few roofs torn in various cities. I opened the radio, similar reports arrived from other countries, the event seemed to have had an epicenter... I started laughing so hard that I hiccupped the rest of the day. Then I opened my email to share the joke with you. A message was waiting for me:

"I want to make love to you. NOOOOOW!" Time – 5:02PM. Huh? My hiccup died, how many O's is three seconds?...

*

night

00:53AM, you: "...in five minutes there's five minutes more since we separated."

00:55AM, I: "...in five minutes there's one hour less until we re-unite."

you: "...sure, same absolute time, just the units change and instead of integers we count fractions."

I: "...no, one absolute hour. Daylight saving time..." I added, looking frightened at the trees. Not even a whiff. Me and my imagination. Though I was a bit disappointed, I expected a bit more excitement your side.

00:59AM, you: "...sorry." Sorry for what?

I'm positively certain the 02:11:40AM solar flare on the other hemisphere had nothing to do with you.

*

nightingale

Spring arrived this morning, at exactly 4:32AM. That's when I sneezed my first of the twenty-three series of sneezes, heralding its arrival in my unbeaten pompous way. I beat the nightingale in accuracy by twenty-three minutes exactly, as its first chirp came at 4:55AM. I wondered if the feat qualified for inclusion in this year's Guinness. At the least for a TV show. You shattered my dream of fame and fortune, when at 07:31AM I opened your 4:30AM email, suavely telling me:

"Spring will arrive at 4:32AM. I feel the vibration in your chest." Damn. At one thousand miles away?

A Round One Hundred Percent Of Lusting Certainty

uncertainty

"When you were born, you were probably innocent?!" It was part statement, part smile, yet did not expect to lose three out of four miserable days to laughter, instead of sex. Yours. The laughter. Ours. The sex. And even afterwards, between sigh and sigh there was the unmistakable guffaw. "What did I say that was so funny?" I finally exploded.

"The *probably*..." you answered, and I did not mind losing the rest of the time, there was not much left anyway. And when you finished your renewed laughter attack, you added, "... and the fact that you are probably wrong."

*

certainty

"All your poetry is about females and sex and lust, what about me?" One of those intimate moments when you felt like complaining.

"You? Aren't you then female and sexy and lustful?" I asked back, winking rhetorically, nevertheless fumbling around under the blankets just to make sure. You allowed me and I got my confirmation, though, instead of enjoying my research into the human genome you spent your time pondering.

"Certainly yes. Am I the only one in your life?" You tried being more specific.

"Certainly not. You are the only woman in my life." I was being very specific.

*

neither

"It's not a typo, is it?" you asked, and as usual I had to answer with a question since I did not really get your meaning.

"Typo what?" I asked back.

"You called your story 'A Round...'.""You didn't mean 'Around...', did you?" Oh, you, and your blessed curls of brain and hair.

"Actually, oops, there is a typo in there..." and you chilled into a shadow in the dying evening's sun. "I said 'Lusting'."

"And?..." and you crisped into an apple-peel in the glaring desert's sun.

"I meant 'Lasting'..." and you lighted into a sunflower in the rising morning's sun.

Archeology

I marked carefully the time in my logbook: 11am, 4th October 2011.

Then picked the bottle with trembling hands and started pulling off the encrusted barnacles and dry seaweed. There was something inside it, for sure. I did not succeed to pull off the cork, so I broke it and let the frail pieces of paper slide into my hand. There were two, one rolled in the other. I spread them on the sand, carefully. The first, had one single word scribbled across it: HELP! The second was a newspaper cut-out, carrying a big title "NEGOTIATIONS FAILED". Dated April, 2023.

One Hundred Princes In Triplicate

kiss

She kissed me so many times that a crocodile would have turned prince. I stayed toad. Rules of legend are not necessarily rules of life. But she wasn't going to give up so easily.

"OK, now *you* kiss me!" Courageously said, but how can a toad kiss when he does not have lips, not even teeth. "French kiss," she insisted, smiling. I did my best. "See?" she croaked happily, crawling out from the pile of clothes that fell limply around her. Actually she said *ribbit ribbit?* but what I heard was *see?*.

We joined tongues and jumped into the pond.

*

kids

I caught a fly and offered it to her. She accepted it graciously.

"You spoil me. One day I will not be able to get off the bottom of the pond." She looked around, proudly. "How will we name them?" she asked, pointing to our thousands of kids. She still carried some endearing human notions.

"Well... toad one, toad two, toad three..." I answered, winking with both eyes. I never succeeded to wink just with one.

"Both the boys and the girls?"

"No, the boys will be toads, the girl toadesses."

"What about the grandchildren?"

Told you, once human...

*

kats

"Cats," she corrected me. Well, a toad is not supposed to be a perfect speller.

"OK, cats. Cats eat toads. Careful, please."

"My cat would never eat me," she stated proudly, pushing the door. I crossed two of my four fingers and followed. The monster lay there, snoring. "Kitty, Kitty..." croaked my lover, jumping on the monster's head.

I've never seen such fangs in my life, the jaws opening wide, ready to snap... luckily I remembered to bring a fish along. We hopped desperately away, poor she crying.

"But... my cat..."

Yeah, catcodile, I spell corrected her in my mind.

The Subject Is So Painful, That It Is Worth 150 Words

doctor

My spine was killing me. A spine is supposed to support you in life, no? Mine was killing me.

I entered the blindingly white, slightly smelling of insecticide, room. I was number 29. When the orthopedist finally accepted me, he examined me and then looked at me, gravely.

"I will have to administer you an epidural infusion."

Cold sweat invaded me. I mean, I wrote stories about it, but this was real life...

"Doctor, am I pregnant?"

For whatever reasons, he made faces as if he was trying hard not to laugh.

"No, Mr. Jones..." (emphasizing the *Mr.*) "...this is not one of your stories..." (aha, finally a fan...) "...and their stupid subjects." (no, not really a fan...) "This is to ease the pain."

I felt as if the entire hospital was making similar faces on my way out. Well, at least it wasn't expensive, even if it didn't help.

*

alternative

I sifted carefully through the "classified", until I found an ad which looked promising.

I pushed the door, which opened with a creaking sound. Several faces looked up from the gloom, frightened. I limped to the computerized tickets dispenser and took a ticket. Again 29, maybe a good omen?

I waited, brooding about nothing, until my number was called.

The cat was sitting on a small, embroidered armchair, looking at me impassively. It wasn't the cat I came to see. Madame Ruth With The Gold-Capped Tooth (her plagiarism, not mine) was sitting on a big, embroidered armchair, surrounded by smells of incense and cat-shit. She smiled at me hugely – the gold tooth real.She thrusted a heavy jeweled hand towards me. I wanted to shake it but she pulled it hastily back.

"First, the money," she blurted crisply.

It cost me five times more than the doctor did. It didn't help.

*

other alternatives

Someone mentioned osteopath. I had nothing to lose but hell.

There were 27 man in the waiting room, one woman. What's that, I brooded, only men suffer back pain? No wonder, sexual discrimination...

I sat down in a comfortable chair, pitying those who arrived after me and had to wait longer.

"Twenty-nine," I heard through my pain mists. She waited for me, standing. A mini-skirt short enough to be called belt, heels long enough to be called stilts, blue eyes to melt the rings of Saturn. "Please, lie down," she invited, emanating jasmin dreams.

I tried not to groan as I lay down on the hard sofa. The view under that mini-skirt, as she worked on my spine, was worth every cent paid.

I relaxed mentally, though I felt certain physical discomfort as I lay on my belly.

It didn't help.

I left, envying all those who arrived after me.

Tried 100 Words, Failed, Still 150. Told You...

It was hell. I gave up on real people and started looking for advice from virtual people, internet. It was endless.

The first was talking about taking vitamin-C by the bucketfull. I had the bucket but where do I get bucketfuls of vitamin-C? The next was talking about camel shit. Mix camel shit with coffee beans, dry, grind and smoke the result. Fine, but there was not one camel a thousand miles around. A third was talking about taking a needle and sticking it... I clicked away before fainting.

Finally I found an intriguing one: send me ten bucks and I make you happy. What the heck, I wasted already hundreds of bucks... paid, and got the link. I clicked it eagerly, there were just two words on the screen: *get laid!!!* With three exclamation marks.

No, it did not slove my problem. But it made me a happy man.

One Hundred Teeth

enamel

"C'mon, lips as sweet as wine?... idiots, dreamers, poets," I said. You looked at me, strangely. "C'mon, nipples as sweet as honey?... idiots, dreamers, poets." You looked at me, stranger still. "C'mon, toes as sweet as sugar-cane?... idiots, etc..." I snorted contemnibly at the ignobility of such unimaginative triteness.

You stopped looking at me, you grabbed me.

Fifteen hours later.

"W wwll swnd www mw dwntwst's bwll," (i.e. "I will send you my dentist's bill") was all I could say with toothless gums, grinning strangely. My mouth's right corner having reached the top of my left ear, and vice versa.

*

porcelain

Of course I did not send you the bill, you could not have paid it. Neither could I, that's why I had to wash his dishes to the end of my days. The dentist's. I smiled.

"What's there in your mouth, you grew new teeth?" you asked.

"Porcelain!" I declared, proudly.

"And you think it will help?" you asked, doubting.

"Guaranteed!" I declared, proudly.

It took thirty hours this time.

"W wwll swnd www mw dwntwst's bwll," (you know what it means, by now). The corners of my mouth reaching back to their place of origin, the long way around.

*

steel

You blinked, blinded.

"Steel, stainless," I said, biting a piece of tram rail and spitting it contemptibly. Not only that, but the dentist had now to wash my dishes to the end of his days, after all the porcelain had been guaranteed.

Sixty hours.

"W wwll nwt swnd www mw dwntwst's bwll," the new word being "not". It was useless anyway. I decided to remain toothless. it had some advantages, after all, like suction power on a variety of bodily structures. Not to mention that facial deformation, that could have been called a grin, touring my head four times around.

One Hundred Bovine Head

encounter

"Hi, mom."

I wasn't her mom. I wasn't even female. And what's worse - she wasn't even human. She was a cow, or rather a calf-almost-cow, grazing peacefully.

"Hi, baby," I muttered, filled with superstitious awe, my natural protective instincts kicking in.

"You think I am crazy?" she asked.

"No, but I certainly am," I answered.

"Save me," she implored, her tail fanning the flies away, "I don't want to finish on Good Morning America." Yes, some fates were worse than death. I had to save her. "Even becoming medium-rare sirloin steak is better," she added, and I started crying.

*

lover

"A talking cow?" she (my lover) asked, holding high the frying pan.

We went to the meadow where she (my lover) fainted. I put her (my lover) on her (the cow's) back and smuggled them into my apartment. Had some problems fitting both in the elevator so first I took her (the cow) upstairs. I had to support her (the cow) as she stood up on her hind feet, to fit better. By the time I got her (my lover) up as well, she (the cow) was snoring gently on the sofa, the TV blaring Heavy Metal.

Yeah, modern kids...

*

money

I had no choice, the neighbors complained we danced, the fly traps cost a fortune, we needed money desperately. I asked her permission, she agreed.

Good Morning America's studios were packed, presenters and public laughing their heads off as I walked Miranda (the cow, not the lover) in.

"So," the presenter choked on his laughter, "you can talk..."

"Moooh..." mooed Miranda, and two hundred spectators rolled. "Cow joke," added Miranda and two hundred spectators, two presenters and several technicians fainted.

I got my ten million dollar contract. Miranda got her farm, my lover got a cat, life was suddenly beautiful.

Jonathan

murder?

"A bug bit me, my elbow is the size of a potato..." she wrote.

"Yeah, a bug called Jonathan," I answered, green with jealousy. She arrived, carrying a huge suitcase, almost man-size. "Jonathan?..." I half joked, eyeing the suitcase suspiciously. She was tight lipped. First we made love like mad dogs, and only then she allowed me to open the suitcase. My fingers were shaking.

There was no blood. Just a huge cage, made of fine, reinforced mesh.

"Jonathana," she made the introductions, stressing the "a", and I watched the giant spider watching me back with hungry, almost intelligent eyes.

*

love?

"Marry me?" I woke up with a start from the dream. "Marry me?" Goodness, it wasn't a dream. I gulped. Well, after Miranda nothing surprised me really.

"You're a spider."

"So what, I'm a widow. And all I need is flies, I don't even need diamonds."

"Yeah, but you might eat me. What about ten million dollars?"

She seemed to consider, her mandibles working.

"Hmm, might be interesting," she finally answered.

"Does she know?" I continued, *she* being my lover.

"No, she would have squashed me." Yes, *she* was that jealous. And with Jonathana's all eight hands tenderly caressing me...

*

wager?

They didn't learn the lesson, this time betting against me ten million dollars, the TV trying to get some money back. They hired a bigger studio, capacity one thousand, ten thousand arrived and riot police was called in. When the show finally started (ten million home-viewers) I brought the cage, and a miniature mike was slid inside it. The presenter was self-confident...

"...you're delusional, spiders possess no vocals - mouth, tongue, cords..." she laughed.

"Just allow my no-vocals between your silicones, you fucking bitch..." Jonathana pipped in impeccable English, as one presenter, one thousand spectators and ten million home-viewers fainted.

Fireman

I was the first to jump from the car. The woman was crying hysterically, pointing to the second floor. I did not wait, rushed up the blazing stairs, found a sobbing baby, picked it and slammed out, breaking the window. Luckily, knowing me, they had the net ready. I broke a leg, the baby was fine, its mom hugged us both, crying. I tried to crawl back for the other but they wouldn't allow me.

I spent the night snapping at my leash and howling at the moon, not in pain, just in knowledge I did not finish my job.

Burglar

job

Ricardo sprung me out of jail three days before my official release. He needed me for an urgent "job" and I was the only one capable to execute it. My fee was one million dollars. One does not argue with one million dollars, even knowing that being caught would be a matter of, at most, days. But my share would go to my wife, allowing her to pay off the huge accumulating hospital debt for our sick kid. Ricardo promised. Ricardo said that Ricardo always kept his word.

I kept my side of the deal. Ricardo did not keep his.

*

sentence

I refused to cooperate with the police, so I was sentenced to ten additional years. Within several months it became clear that Ricardo was not going to keep his promise. It was not my job to implicate him, my grudge irrelevant. I left it to the cops.

Less then one year later, my daughter passed away at home. There was no money to hospitalize her. Inside one month my wife committed suicide. I did not cry. I just locked myself in a wall inside a wall, of silence, sat in my cell and waited for the ten years to pass.

*

verdict

They let me go at the end of seven years, on grounds of exemplary behaviour. They even gave me some honestly earned money.

First, I visited the graves with fresh flowers. Then I visited a friend. Then I bought a chic suit, went to the restaurant and asked for their most expensive wine. By the time Ricardo arrived with his distinguished art collectors, I had finished it. I got up, went to his table and shot him through the forehead.

They sentenced me to the chair, on grounds of premeditation. For once in my life, I agreed with the establishment.

Eyesight

You sent me pictures from the event.

"My editor is the beautiful, smiling woman," you wrote, "and the pretty girls played guitar during my reading. The gorgeous blonde with the big boobs, is the mayor, the boobs are real – I saw her once bathing." I swallowed hard, blinked... "The other blonde, hugging me, is my doctor. Gorgeous, no? And the..." ...going on and on, for two full pages.

I started sweating, squirming frightened. My God, something was terribly wrong with my eyesight. I needed a doctor, urgently. You see, all I could see was you. Even with my eyeglasses on.

Cleopatra

I had a horrible dream. I was Cleopatra's lover.

So, what was so horrible about it?

She was beautiful, a painting, a goddess, something between Greta Garbo to Liz Taylor to Jessica Simpson - voice, body, face... Though she was slightly diastematic.

What's that? Something like diabetic?

No, something like a gap between teeth.

Is that all? So what? So has Topol, minus the voice, minus the body, minus the face. What was so horrible about it?

No, not this was the problem. The problem was that the dream started too late.

???

It started when they started mummifying me.

Hundreds Of Squirrels

blue

Her ass was blue.

"Your ass is blue," I said.

"How do you know?" she asked, her teeth competing with the squirrels. They, at least, were breaking nuts.

"X-Ray vision," I joked. She was frozen, icicles probably hanging from her brain's convolutions.

"Please... make it Infra-Red?..."

"Okay," I said, "but for that, you have to be naked."

She started undressing middle of the street. Yeap, icicles. I had to pull up her trousers and drag her home by force, as she kept trying... By the time we arrived, even the squirrels were laughing, making movements of rolling down their pants.

*

red

"No... really?" she blushed, lying naked and allowing my hands do the blue to red job. By then most of her brain icicles had thankfully melted away.

"Look," I said, allowing a squirrel that sneaked in perform the pants down pantomime.

"Knickers too?" she asked, cheeks suddenly redder than ass.

"Yes," I snickered. She gasped. "At home." She relaxed.

The squirrel tried to get some attention, biting my hand. I shooed it away. Hey, I am not that perverse, mate. She tried to get some attention too, biting my hand too. Well... okay... hey, I am not *that* innocent either.

*

neither blue nor red

"I was frozen, I must have had icicles hanging from my brain," she laughed. Okay, she said it which made it... okay. "So what's the color of my ass now?" she whispered, nuzzled, snuggled... I couldn't see, not with the squirrel sleeping, belly up, all over it.

"White... I guess?"

"Guessing won't get you first prize," was her turn to snicker.

Well, had no choice, had to disturb the poor squirrel. Though the first prize, was worth all the bites I got on all my extremities. And I do mean ALL. Well, I did find succor for one, at least.

One Hundred And The One Pills

"Did you take your pills?"

"Which pills?"

"Okay, I see, you did not take them. Here... 1, 2, 3... 42, 43."

"Did *you* take *your* pill?"

"Pill?"

"Yes, the one that counts."

"A counting pill?"

"You *are* getting senile. Counts, like important." She was right, it was probably all those pills I was taking, now at one hundred and one and growing. My memory was working though not the rest. Especially not *that*. I needed *that* pill. For her it was the other way around - *that* was the *only* thing that *was* working.

I took the pill. It worked.

*

"I didn't see Jonathan here lately. He probably forgot to take his pills."

"He did not, I gave them to him."

"So how come he didn't come?" She made it sound like cum. That really pissed me off. Jonathan was her previous lover, when she was younger. Seventy eight.

"Maybe because I gave him the pills," I spit venomously, stressing the *because*.

She looked up, appalled. Well, ninety three does you something. Then she got it, and beckoned to me, smiling.

A knock at the door. It was Jonathan. Shit, just when I was getting ready to take *my* pill.

*

She kept moaning, and meowing, and ohhh'ing and ahhh'ing, the only thing she didn't do was write it on my chest. And I couldn't find that damn pill. Unless if that damned Jonathan... no, at two hundred and two pills... no chance. I was about to cry or shoot myself when I found it, with my spare teeth. Hooray... I washed it down and hurried to the bed.

"And now, what do I do?" she asked.

She clearly didn't take her pills. I didn't give a damn, all I had was one shot. She was going to learn from experience.

Of All The One Hundred Countries On Record...

"I have a surprise for you," I said, seating her on my knees.

"Yes?..." she shivered, eyes shining with expectation She didn't even touch me there where she usually did.

"I'm taking you to dreamland..."

"Yes?..." she repeated breathlessly, watching me the way a pagan worshiper watches her stone idol. Trust me, that stone idol had a lot to envy me for.

""I am taking you to... Albania."

She fainted. Oh, my God, I should not have done it. I didn't expect her to react in such beautiful, emotional way. She would never forgive me for the about to come.

*

She recovered, tears in her eyes, powerful emotions still burning deep down there.

"Albania?..." her voice choking... oh, how I hated to disappoint her... oh, poor girl, oh, bastard me. But I had no choice.

"Oh, forgive me, love, no, but another place. The good thing is that it also starts and ends with A."

"America?" she screamed in panic. I had to calm her before the next faint.

"No, baby, no, don't worry - Anglia."

"Anglia?..." The disappointment after Albania was so distressing... She sensed my distress and did her best to calm me, kissing me like a madwoman.

*

"Anglia... there's no such country," she chirped, gently punishing me for cheating her out of the Albanian dream.

"Well, there is, you see..." I tried to appease her, feeling very small in a very big hole, "...it's a sub-kingdom in the United Kingdom. And they still believe in fairytales there - like their queen never pees. And they are also technologically very advanced - they developed two taps: one for cold water and one for warm water..." I kept on mumbling, trying to soothe her wound.

I think she finally forgave me, the way she over-compensated that night with sex.

Onomatopoeically Yours

"Johnny, dog!"

"Woof-woof-woof." Sure, easy. Next card...

"Squirrel!" He hesitated.

"Squirrel-squirrel-squirrel?..." I ROFLed for three hours, up just once for a pee, then sat in front of him, hiccupping.

"You're a riot, boy. And this?..." ...a cow card.

"Cow-cow-cow..." He waited for me to finish ROFLing again, before conceding... "okay - moooh..." He couldn't grin, but I was sure he was grinning. I raised a cat card...

"Grrr..." yeah, this was stretching it too much.

"Okay, let's go," I said, picking the leash. Johnny is my dog. We keep it secret. No, not the fact that he's a dog.

Man Woman Continuum

"Man is the natural enemy of life."

"Man, you say, meaning not woman." Her logic had the habit of driving me insane.

"Woman is the natural enemy of man. Thus, implied by inclusive extrapolation it is also the natural enemy of life." I was using big words, trying to confuse her. I did not.

"Or the other way around." Sure, she was right, it could be small eaten by big who is eaten by bigger, or my enemy's enemy is my friend. *"And I?"* she insisted further.

"We! you mean. We... are neither. We are... *lovers!"*

She kissed me. Passionately.

*

"For a moment there, I thought you were a man," she laughed, her hand making sure I knew that she knew what I was.

"For a moment there, a similar thought crossed my mind," I tried from behind the safety of plagiarism.

"About me, or about you? Being a man, I mean?" Hmmm... linguistically speaking she was correct, my statement was not really defined. I had no choice and let my hand do something similar. To her. I believe this removed any doubt of misinterpretation. Funny how imperfect a language devoid of physical manifestation can be.

She kissed me. Passionately.

*

"Let's swap roles," I dared.

"You mean the woman-man thing?"

"I mean the man-woman thing."

"You mean in the world?"

"I mean in the bed."

"You mean we? You mean I and you, separately?"

"I mean I... you, you, I, I mean together... ahm... separately..." was it the onset of exasperation or Alzheimer's?

"You mean this?" Being quite shy, I couldn't really answer. *"Or this?"* I couldn't answer this one either. *"Or maybe... this?"* I was chocking. *"I thought you'd never ask,"* she smirked, and although I didn't remember asking anything... the answer was appropriately overwhelming.

She kissed me. Passionately.

Lotto

I chose the numbers, carefully. Ninety million Euros is serious business and I had to get my six numbers right or miss this unique opportunity. Lotto is unforgiving, as you know.

I read the three Nostradamus volumes I owned, one in Latin that I didn't quite understand. Then I read the full Statistics Encyclopedia, went to the gypsy at the street corner for a garlic (heavily) flavored advice, threw thirty times one-Euro coins in a fountain over my left shoulder, spit three times east... I was ready. I didn't win.

Probably I should have spit seven times. Well, next time.

*

"And if you won, what would you have done with it?" she asked, her pitiful laughter... pitiless. This kind of question I had no problems with.

"I would buy me the sneakers which they wanted ninety euros for, during sales. Maybe even two pairs. Also five white t-shirts with an Elvis picture. Fly to Tirana, just to get the one missing stamp in my passport, go to the silk-worms museum, buy a course in knitting, maybe also knitting needles of unbreakable plastic..."

"You are crazy, you know?" she sighed.

"Why? I am rich, I can do anything I want, no?"

*

I won. Told you, should have spit seven times. Seventy-five millions only, still good enough for my dreams. Bought the t-shirts, bought the sneakers, spent two days in jail in Tirana but got my stamp... She didn't believe me, even when I showed her the stamp.

"You are crazy, you know?" she sighed, *"where's the Porsche, the diamond studded watch, the...?"*

"Wait, wait, now the big surprise, my BIG dream," I smiled smugly, pulling the tiny, laced panties from the gift package.

"This? Your BIG dream?" she choked.

"No. Pull them up. My big dream is to... pull them down."

Alien

"...then at breakfast I turned over the butter and it was written: contains milk. Ha-ha-ha, what next? On a bottle of Bordeaux - contains wine, on a skirt - contains woman, on a nipple..."

"...contains acid."

"Huh?!"

She unholstered her zapper, pulled the shirt strap down, pulled the brassiere strap down...

"You can bet your life on it." Bet my life? Damn my life!... I attacked, bit, sucked, licked... I heard her laugh... "How did you know?"

"I didn't. I did not care."

Her eyes coruscated.

"I never believed I would ever say it to a human. I love you."

OMG!

I woke up to terrible noise, babble, babble, sounded like gossip about bird-poop and worms and damn cats may they burn in hell... I stumbled over to the window and opened it upon a view of hundreds of flying swallows... OMG!... I suddenly understood Swallowish?

I shook awake my wife, she opened one lazy eye asking... asking? She was barking. I stumbled backwards, sweating, wiped my brow with a shaky hand then looked at my palm - at the soft, small, lazily undulating feather there.

OMG! I unfurled long wings and flew outside, leaving some kind of scream behind me.

Vitamins et Co.

C et Co.

"...and C contributes to collagen and red lycopen antioxidizes and pink astaxanthin fights keratoses as well as radicals, rogues and communists, not to mention lutein..." I was set on my long, daily health speech, just about to settle comfortably on the bed for the coming hour, when she interrupted me.

"And this?" Okay, since this is no video, I can only mention that she took hold of an important piece of humanity, which had nothing to do with vitamins.

"This?" I gulped.

"I need this vitamin, NOW!" she squeezed. It left me no choice but to obey. Reluctantly. (*Yeah, sure...*)

*

A et Co.

"...and A can be found in a variety of forms, as retinol in meats and as several carotenes in vegetables, all of which are converted to the retinal that... you yawn?"

"Yes, sorry love, this is extremely intelligent yet extremely boring."

"Also extremely important," I insisted, "for a healthy life you must eat your liver and your sweet potato and your carrot..." she streched suddenly, languidly...

"Oh, carrot?... mmm... I love carrot..." she smiled, blinking her vitamin A flooded eyes and stretching her hand my way, downwards, proving she completely misinterpreted it. But, hey, once she reached there... who cared?

*

D et Co.

"...and D is good for bones systems, for immunity systems..."

"For sex systems?" She had this one track mind, following this same dead-end-street ending always at this same dead-end which, at a certain stage, I did not mind reaching as well.

"Nothing proven. And our body synthesizes it independently by UVB light..."

"Like this?..." she turned the night lamp on.

"... on exposed body parts..."

"Like this?..." she pulled my zipper down.

"...and butter is sometimes artificially fortified with it...

"Like this?..." She started peeling a butter package.

"...like what?"

I was clearly in no condition to continue my exposé.

Beads

She passed through the glass door, as if there was no glass, the beads rolling on the floor behind her. I followed, collecting each bead, even the crushed ones, until I reached the glass. There were beads beyond it, all the way to the airplane's escalator. I could not follow, though I tried again and again, banging my head against the armored glass until a couple of white uniforms dragged me away.

A blue uniform followed, wiping the blood stains from the glass. Sharp bead shards started cutting through my deeply pocketed fists as I crushed, and crushed, and crushed...

Slavery

She dragged me to the shower, opened the tap, closed the door, closed her eyes and started singing. I had to do the hard work - started lathing softly at the neck, rubbing smoothly down to shoulders, alongside ribs in long languorous movements, between breasts, under breasts, around breasts advancing suggestively towards nipples... nipples... nipples... mmmmm... oops, almost slipped, saved in the nick of time as I continued lower down towards the belly, between her thighs... thighs... thighs... yesss... mmmmm... heaven... oh!... nooo!... hell!... as she turned off the water, wrapped me in paper and dropped me in the bin.

Sweet Wine, A Bottle Of Beer, And A... Jap

sweet wine

"Which would you prefer? Dry, semi-dry, sweet?"

"Sweet."

I saw only one bottle. She opened it, poured a glass and handed it to me.

"Here."

I eyed her defiantly - was she some Cassandra? - before tasting.

"It's not sweet," I complained. She lay on her back and filled her navel with the wine.

"Try now." My goodness, it was sweet. I smiled.

"I guess it is all here," and I pointed to the piece of my anatomy hanging above my neck.

"No, here," she said, pointing to a piece of my anatomy hanging elsewhere.

Well, she was probably half-right.

*

bottle of beer

"Which would you prefer? Heineken, Carlsberg, Stella?"

"*Stella.*"

I opened the one unlabelled bottle and handed it to her.

"Here."

She eyed me defiantly then drank.

"*Blahhh, Coke,*" she said. I lay on my back and filled my navel with the liquid.

"Try now." She tried.

"*Blahhh, still Coke.*" I scratched my head, feeling at a loss.

"I guess women are different there," and I pointed to the piece of my anatomy hanging above my neck.

"*Yes, but the same there,*" she said, pointing to a piece of her anatomy (not hanging) elsewhere.

Well, she proved she was fully right.

*

tap

"In your opinion, which direction do I open this tap for wine and which direction for beer?"

"*In my opinion you are an idiot. Both directions are water.*"

"Wanna bet?"

"*No problem. On my body. And if I win?*"

"A diamond ring."

I opened the tap to the right and filled a glass. Then opened to the left and filled another glass, handing her both. She sipped from the first, then sipped from the second. Then she eyed me strangely. She had no choice.

The best spent dollars of my life. Hey, don't worry, she got also the ring. After.

Eyeglasses

"Why do you put them on?" I asked her, surprised. Her sight was perfect.

"To better see you," she said.

"Aha, I see, and the next one will be *to better hear you*, followed by *to better smell you*, and ending with *to better eat you*." I shivered, then complemented it with a wink.

"I think it was the wolf, not the girl saying those things, no?" she smiled back with condescending apprehension.

"This is a modern egalitarian world," I countered, watching her sticking a contraption in her ear. "And what's this one for?"

"To better hear you," she said...

Pendant

What are the three circles hanging to the chain around your neck? I asked.

You should know, she answered, smiling indulgently. *The outer one is my breast.*

Your breast? It wasn't going the way I thought. I touched her breast and watched it melt into puddles of sun.

The inner one is my spine, she continued unperturbed, leaving me with a frown. I touched her spine, watching it melt into puddles of sunflower.

And the in-between, is it your heart? I chuckled, wondering how to touch it.

The in-between is you, she finished, watching me melt into puddles of flesh.

Baby Powder

chapter one

"Can you please bring me the baby-powder?" she murmured. We barely knew each other, yet we were in love, madly.

I watched her, obliquely.

"Something naughty on your mind?" I brought it over, even opened it for her, smilingly expecting lust, debauchery...

She undressed shamelessly naked... *"thank you..."* broke the box completely and threw the powder in the air creating a cloud, disappeared into it... I heard the window opening and watched in awe the gigantic white butterfly taking to the skies...

"No," I screamed, rushing into the cloud myself, emerging on the other side... still human. I lost her.

*

chapter two

I do not believe in fairies. Nor in witches, extra-terrestrials, hallucinations. She was real. We made love, I still carried the scar on my lip. She disappeared. Three years ago. I kept the window open, whatever she was - angel, demon - I wanted her back, I was melting away in pain and longing. I kept the leftovers of baby-powder... why? Why did I agree to take it out of her bag and give it to her instead of flushing it down the drain, damn me? Another day. She did not return. I switched off the light and fell asleep.

*

chapter three

I sneezed, waking up. She sat on the bed, watching me cross-legged, naked, a sunshine middle of the night. The leftovers of the powder box in her right hand.

"Do you want to know?" she asked. I knew my life depended on the answer, I knew what my answer was.

"No," I answered.

She got up, turned on the tap and pushed the box underneath it. I watched the powder melt, disappear. She returned to the bed.

"I love you," she said, and all I could do was bask in the endless pain of cuts she inflicted upon my lips.

Dough

Dough one

"Mama, where is Gretel?"

"Gone into the woods."

"Oh, no, didn't she read the story?..." I rush away.

"Hansel!..." calls mama but I do not halt, I have to save Gretel. I follow the bread crumbs, reach the witch's house and there, thankfully, I see Gretel kneading dough.

"Hansel, can you help me, I ate some of the wall and now I have to repair it.

"Thank God, she did not eat you..."

"C'mon, Hansel, you don't really believe that story?" she laughs. I watch the gingerbread walls, sugar window-panes... well...

"Gretel, help me with the fire?..." calls a voice.

*

Dough two

She bends over the fresh dough and presses her breasts in. Then straightens inspecting the result, pensive.

"Why did you do it?" I ask, licking sticky leftovers from her nipple.

"I have to win that bread design competition."

"No chance," I laugh, "they all create castles, demons, ships. Most of them come from sand sculpting."

"Everybody forgets one thing," she counters, trying to steal back from my mouth the leftovers I snatched earlier on. It ends... you know how.

"Which is?" I ask later, panting.

"The judges are all men."

She won. It was not the breasts she finally used.

*

dough three

"How much flour?" I shout.

"Plenty," he shouts back, above the mixers' noise.

"Yeast?"

"Plenty," he shouts impatiently, fooling with that new red-head. Well, I am but the apprentice and don't want to lose my job...

The Herald

West Road had to be evacuated as unprecedented disaster hit this peaceful street. A sci-fi sized fresh-dough Blob poured out of Jake's Bakery, swallowing everything on its way. Police investigates. Experts still evaluate the damage to the environment.

I found a new job, in a fireworks factory.

"How much Ammonium Nitrate?" I shout.

"Plenty," he shouts back, fooling with the new brunette.

Of Course... Family

Napoleone

Tyrant. Female. Not reaching my waist and weighing less than a watermelon, yet controlling my life.

"Gramps, now you're baby, I'm mommy. I will pick you up." She fails, NOT because I'm overweight. "Now sit in the trolley..." ...the puppet trolley. It shatters, NOT because I'm overweight. "Now let's wrestle." One hour later I crack any vertebra still intact and add a second crack to those already cracked.

"Okay, now let's nap," I try limiting the damage, betting that in ten she'll be asleep and I can return to my beloved PC.

I lose, of course. In five I'm asleep.

*

Kasparovish

Her big brother. Hmm... big... reaching my chest and shattering my chess pride each time we play. Such impertinence. Well, it is about time I teach the little brat a lesson, no?

"Gramps, let's play."

"Sure," I snicker, having been coached secretly for the last five months by one of Kasparov's old trainers, having memorized one year of games books with help of a hypnotist, and now having a webcam fixed on the board with a CIA ear-plug in my ear and my coach guiding me remotely, hehe... I even let him play the white.

"e2-e4..."

I lose, of course.

*

Tommylike

Then there's this other of the small monsters, the one in between. No, he didn't see the Who's Tommy, and he isn't dumb-deaf-blind and he has no Pinball machine but he has a damn Wii machine... goodness, the dust that I bite.

"I have a present for you," I smile mischievously, unwrapping my old Atari. "Care to play?" I don't tell him I've been Space Invaders town champion, and second place at the country championships. To secure my position even more I also give him the joystick with the defective shooting button.

Of course, you know by now. I lose.

*

At the risk of crossing the sacrosanct 100 barrier... who the hell needs such offspring? I ask. Well, I guess that... I. Of course.

Comb Magic

six

I counted its teeth as it went into her hair - six. Counted again when it went out - four. What the hell? Started looking for the stray teeth, they were nowhere to be found. Tried again - three. One. None. Frightening.

"Love..." I started, hesitating. She moaned, turning languidly around.

"I had a strange dream, you combed my hair..." I felt like fainting... "then the comb teeth..." I fainted.

I woke up, counting sixty-six teeth on the comb in my hand. Strange dream, I thought, counting the pearls on her neck. Six. I could swear there were none before.

*

sixty-six

"You're crazy," she said, looking at me obliquely. "I wish there were sixty-six, though," she smiled. Oh, decide woman, crazy or... I picked the sixty-six toothed comb and started combing. Sixty. Fifty-two... Twelve. None.

I fainted, why wait? I also woke up, inspecting her neck (usually it was her breasts). Sixty-six diamonds, counted. "Something wrong?" she asked, sparkling like all the fires of hell. I looked at the comb in my hand, counted. Six-hundred-sixty-six. I fainted again, for safety. When I woke up I found her parading in front of the mirror. At least she did not call me crazy.

*

six-hundred-sixty-six

"You're crazy." Hmm, she did after all. I probably was. Suddenly I didn't mind. So maybe she was the devil, so what? She was a woman, no? I didn't see the difference. I started combing her hair, no comb-tooth falling this time, after three strokes she started purring, after fifteen... "Love, make love to me..." she murmured, throwing the comb away and grabbing me. I did. "Love, make love to me..." she murmured. I did. "Love, make love..." I did. "Love..." I did... I did...

Guess how many times. I'll give you a hint - it ends with a six.

Perfume Of The Day

The clouds invade, attack... oh, goodness, another office day. I choke on the sweetish, heavy feminine haze around my desk and stumble breathlessly towards the men's-room, even this would be a respite. Yes, before I get in, then stumble back out even before closing my fly, a degenerating mix of purging smells asphyxiating me. Why the hell don't everybody eat same food? I totter back to my desk... Soup? (with morning?) Steak?? (huh??) Sex??? (what???)... God!!! I scream, save me!!!...

Oh, finally, thank You for listening... a refreshing, gentle breeze of after-shave... I crawl after it avidly...

"Hi," she smiles.

Re-Creative

She had this one-letter associative mania. This day looked like her *re* day.

"I coined a new word," she smiled, "*repolution.*"

"Wrong," I reacted. "First: revolution originates from Latin *revolutio*, *re* in the root, pollution from *pollutus*, no *re* in the root. Second: it should have two l's. Third: it's meaningless."

"Okay," she conceded easily, "then what about *recocknition?*" As I eyed her strangely, she hastened "*repubican? repission? recrapitulate?* I have definitions..."

This was going too far.

"What about we *repopulate* that small brain of yours with nicer words and images?" I suggested, holding her tighter.

"You mean... ahmm... *recopulate?*"

A Chocolatean... Conscience

...white

"This is NOT chocolate," I insisted, refusing to put it on the shelves under my responsibility. "It is cocoa-fat and some other sugary stuff, but no cocoa liquor content. I will not cheat my customers. Fire me!" I was just three days in the job and was already clashing with my supervisor.

"Okay, you're fired," he said, scribbling furiously.

Same evening I went to the store manager to get my payoff.

"You work in a supermarket, you know?" she said, reading.

"Yes, ma'am."

"And you said *my customers*, correct?"

"Yes, ma'am."

I got one chocolate bar. White. And a promotion.

*

...milk

"...so you're a cocoa worshiper?" she asked, mystified.

"No, of Ek Chuah. And we're now in Muán so I will not go for less than 25% cocoa liquor. Even here in the states." I was also the production manager.

"The difference between 10% and 25% is a hefty 16 million dollars additional expense for this... ahmm... Muán month, you know? And this is Hershey's."

"Is he a god?"

She was the factory director. She signed it off. We knew we were both going to get fired. Sales took off with 25 million additional profits. We were promoted. We also married.

*

...dark

"Minimum 70%. Then I will advertise for you the flavonoids and the catechins and its assumed healthy anti-oxidative effects. Not before. We'll do it for free. Make the calculation." I represented a business but was also a health nut. They calculated fast and signed the contract.

My company had no choice but to respect it. They also fired me.

They called me back, offering me the same position for triple the commission when my president got the Presidential Citizens Medal, based on that ad. I accepted, only after they forced the manufacturer to add on each package: *toxic to dogs*.

Prescription

I had an eyeglasses prescription, went to Angloshvili, the local optician. Got a great deal but he remarked on my limp, giving me a letter to Belgoshvili, an orthopedist he knew. Belgoshvili sold me shoe inserts but due to my paleness, he referred me to a hepatologist, Congoshvili, great doctor. Sure, I knew of my acne, and Denmoshvili did an outstanding job. By the time I got to Indoshvili I got x-rayed, endoscoped, acupunctured, operated... I got suddenly suspicious. High IQ, you know...

On my way to Japoshvili I opened the last reference letter: *"only $30,451 to our yacht, yippeee..."*

Harassment

She charged me with everything from seduction through abduction to finally rape. Now I was facing a HR committee, headed by Jake, with intent to terminate me... "...*John, better leave quietly, no pay, no nothing, otherwise...*" Whatever I claimed they rejected, always crashing against "...*Rachel this, Rachel that...*"

They left me no choice except bringing cold proof. I started undressing.

"Huh?" they ogled with disbelief my breasts, belly, lower down... "Then why did she?..."

"Now, why don't you ask Rachel to undress?" I rebuked, re-buttoning myself.

When she refused, Jake, impertinently, groped her groin.

"Huh?" He turned very sickly green.

One Hundred And Fifty Mutants, As I Dreamt Them

tickler

I tickled her cat to purr. Then her dog to sleep three days, her cow to more milk, her goat to more cheese, her cherry tree to pitless cherries. It was snowing at the time. I even tickled her bed to sprout buds, though they dried immediately for lack of nourishment.

"Are you a whisperer or something?" she asked, awed.

"Tickler," I answered.

"ET?" she continued her investigation.

"Why? Am I as ugly as she was?" I laughed.

"She? How do you know it was a she?" she reacted, suddenly suspicious, upset. Urgent damage control was necessary so I tickled her into forgetting, then into forgiving, then into forgetting the *for* in forgiving. I didn't tickle her into milk, her dry nipples were delicious *au naturel*.

"Please..." she begged, shuddering down for the seventy-seventh time and starting up the seventy-eighth.

Well, since anyway the nipple was already in my mouth...

*

twister

I was in trouble. Everything I touched with my right fingertips started twisting clockwise, everything with the left counterclockwise. I was a freak. Sure, it carried advantages. I didn't need a drilling machine, a screwdriver, and when someone upset me all I had to do was touch some part of his anatomy. But I had to use my knuckles to type, and my fist to hold a fork, and as far as women... life was hell.

I worked in an ironmongery, twisting bars for fences. And she was so beautiful... "Come," she said," dragging me to her car, door, bedroom. "Touch," she said, and first her buttons twisted and tore, then her elastics... "Touch," she said, pointing to her nipple. I was about to scream in despair, when she took my right and left index fingers, joined them and... touched.

Oh, the wisdom of that girl, oh, that virginal pleasure...

*

troubleshooter

The best. Fact. First, simple devices, then complex devices, then I discovered I could repair/solve anything. Extrapolating into social situations, political conflicts... any type of problem. There was a condition, though. Both problem and solution had to include an 'a'. Crazy, no? Fact. I was most probably an alien. A gentle one.

I landed in Dubai and was whiskered straight to sheikh Abdul-Ahad. "This is sheikh Musa. My son kidnapped his daughter. They were caught, both have to die. Please, save them."

"Names?"

"Munir." Bad. "Aisha." Perfect.

I rode into Musa's camp dragging two boxes. Musa and his elders waited.

Click!

"One is diamonds. One is an A-bomb. If you move any... bang! I leave with the two kids. Once in London you get the code."

I sent the code. One diamonds. One pure lead. Told you, probably an alien.

The kids called their first born A. Just in case.

Publishers

His daughter let me in, guiding me to his room. He sat rocking on a big chair, Hamlet in his hand, several other books on the table next to him - Tolstoy, Twain, Poe... She pointed to these.

"His only connection to the world. Reads only these, again and again."

I approached, picked his poetry book from the desk and put it under his nose.

"One of the best, ever," he mumbled, returning to Hamlet.

"Damn world and publishers," she sighed, "waited for his Alzheimer's to hit before granting him the Pulitzer."

Publishers? Sharks, I thought bitterly, closing the door.

around... 100

I put on the slippers she bought me.

"Look, I said, there's a defect, one is blue and one is black."

She watched me, lengthily.

"You're an idiot, you know. I bought you two pairs. Go bring the other pair, I bet they're also one blue and one black."

I didn't quite get what this had to do with being an idiot. I was about to get up when it dawned on me, pity suddenly welling up in my heart.

"Oh, poor girl, you're color blind."

She screamed and left me. I guess she couldn't bear me knowing her secret.

*

around... 75

"Eighty feet, that's how many dogs?"

She was suspicious.

"Is this a trick question?"

"No trick question."

"Dogs or cats?"

"Does it matter?"

"To me it does."

"Dogs."

She wrinkled her nose.

"Big?"

"Gigantic," I almost screamed.

"When?"

"Jesus..." my fists opening and closing, eager to strangle something, "fifteen BC."

Her eyes lighted with holy knowledge.

"Hehe, gotcha, there was no Jesus BC."

I screamed and left her. I guess I couldn't bear it, period.

*

around... 50

She was a whore.

"Virgin?" I asked.

"Yes, and so's your mom," she answered politely, undressing.

"What's that?" I asked, inspecting her groin.

"That's where children come from, nitwit."

"John. And you're mistaken," I opened my wallet showing her my stork. She screamed, running away with my wallet. Ahh, innocence...

Talk

We married. At 4:16pm she started talking. She never stopped since.

All seven times we had sex she talked about the curtains, all seven births, between screams, she told the doctors about pickles, when our daughters got married she held elocutions about Tolstoy all seven marriages, when she slept she never slept, when she shut up she never shut up... heeelp!!!

On our fiftieth anniversary I asked her five minutes of quiet to allow for the mayor's speech. She filed for divorce and married our neighbor. Lucky guy. He is deaf.

I married the mayor. At 5:22pm she started talking.

A Scale'ing Matter

I weighed 300pounds. Everyone called me fatso, except mom. She called me chubby. Laura weighed 80pounds. Anorexic. She loved me. Everybody called us Laura and Hardy, me being Hardy. I loved her. She was always on top.

We decided to save each other, meet halfway. We did. I reached 80 and she 300, but she still preferred on top. It turned to a life and death matter.

We decided to meet halfway again. Mom offered us an accurate scale, we were delighted to have reached a satisfying weight of 150.

"Hardy," asked Laura watching the scale, "does kilo mean anything?"

Brainwave

"*You heard, we have a hippopotamus in our head?*"

"No, love, you have a hypothalamus."

"*What's the difference?*"

"Size, for one."

"*So what's the big deal? Also my tits are bigger than yours and it doesn't bother me.*" But I could sense her hurt.

"It bothers *me*, in a *positive* way." I emphasized everything that needed emphasis, trying to assuage her feelings.

She hesitated.

"*Is also my hypothalamus the bigger thing?*"

I hesitated as well, just a moment.

"No, love, I don't think there is place for one inside your skull."

She batted beautiful eyes my way.

"*Thank you, love.*"

Capacity

She was expecting guests, they were meeting in a restaurant.

"Eat a lot, love, especially if they pay," I winked. She hugged me, almost apologetically.

"You know my limited capacity," she laughed and she kissed me.

"Your limited capacity?" I raised an inquisitive eyebrow. I proved the opposite. Easily.

"Love, this is not what I meant," she smirked, sliding away. The sound of running water was almost blasphemous.

Well, dear reader, if by now *you* don't know what I meant, then this whole book was wasted on you. Are you sure there is place for a hypothalamus inside *your* skull?

Fourrourou

Six months at sea was too much, even for me. I entered the "Golden Hand", the port's massage parlor, for some relief. Not a respectable establishment, yet respectful. The gap-toothed bouncer smiled big... "Chaste Maria developed something new, just for you... fourrourou."

Oh, talented, soft, inventive Maria. One hour later I was a squirming mass of delight.

Six grueling driving hours and I was home, barged in and kissed wildly my woman.

"Now..." I smiled mischievously, "...fourrourou."

One hour later she was a squirming mass of delight. The she pulled my ear, whispering...

"And now, can we have some sex?..."

Premonition

She punched the keyboard with her nose.

"What happened?" I screamed, rushing over.

"This horrible dream... my wash-machine died and I washed by hand, my hands withered, died... I used my nose... oh, God... was just trying it..."

"You silly," I laughed, inspecting her fingers, nevertheless.

Three days later she phoned.

"My wash-machine died and I..." Oh, no! I dropped the phone and drove like a maniac... *"...just installed a new one,"* she finished into the dead line, gaping up at me.

"I thought..."

"You silly," she laughed. I didn't have to inspect her fingers, they started their own inspection.

Ghost...s

I did not believe in ghosts. Before. Before my dish-washer went surprisingly on strike, before it turned itself on without reason, same the kettle, then the vacuum-cleaner, the TV, the... what the hell was going on? I opened yellow pages, chose ghostbuster sixty-one, Mamba, and chewed my nails waiting for the results.

I paid in advance, for his black cat too. They sniffed my electricity, poured some syrup, scribbled (the man), growled (the cat), meowed (both), suddenly they both bolted and ran away, screaming, Mamba looking strangely pregnant.

I guess they've encountered a new ghost. This time my kettle disappeared.

The One Hundred (Thousand) Mosquitoes'...
Insanity

species

There is a new species around - they don't zzzzz, they just do their thing and then disappear, leaving behind that horrible itch. I bought an ultra-sound, a vaporizing-container, a high-voltage-zapper... all I got was an intoxication and a zapped finger. And I can't hear anymore the highs in Aida. Damn. I will win, I am the human, the master.

I bought a hammer. Works. Had to replace some windows at home, though. Also some car windshields. There was this mosquito on my neighbor's nose...

Wait, the door bell... I wonder what those big guys in white are looking for...

*

fatherhood

Oh, no, I just found out that I fathered this night about 600 mosquito babies - three bites and one female and I am father to a nation. The bitch. And imagine none of them are eaten by frogs, a few months later I am father to millions, billions... I wonder - do they call me God, the moment before the frog's tongue lashes out? This might be the way to human salvation - imagine that my first commandment to them will be: *thou shalt not bite.*

I wonder why the white haired doctor shakes her head. Probably in admiration.

*

calculus

If one mosquito draws 0.01 milliliter blood, biting ten times would be 0.1 milliliter. Ten thousand mosquitoes would thus draw 1 liter blood, ten million - 1000 liter. Now - that's farming for you, Dracula. A few mosquito-hives and you're set.

Dracula tries vainly to untie his jacket sleeves, I guess he wants to go into farming right away. *Nurse,* I call, but the giant redhead nurse doesn't pay attention, wiggling the keys while humming Maxwell's Silver Hammer. You will, oh, you will, I smile inside, caressing lovingly the little hammer snuggly lining my pocket.

If one silver hammer bangs...

The Three Mousquitors

the linguist

...mind you, we're millions of years old. We evolved from *zzzz* down to *zzz* and some even *z/2*. One specimen (Moquitowitz, Israel) went the other way, up to *zzzzzzzz:* We enriched our language geographically, in France with *miam-miam*, in South-Africa *lekka-lekka* and in Anglo-Saxia *finga-licka-good*... quite a mouthful this one, when our mouths are not full, hehe.

Our elders (three weeks old, sometimes four) claim to have sucked poetry while sucking blood, no pun intended, realizing verses type *zzz-z-z-miamalekkamiama-z-z-meow*. The last element from a dog. What's a cat?

Do you know a publisher?

Ouch, you bwoke my pwoboscis, *y-y-y-y-yuman*...

*

the leftist

...love everybody. Dogs, cows, men, lizards, women. So what if we're female? Gay pride. A, B, O, Rhesus or no Rhesus... who cares for Erythroblastosis-Fetalis? Why isn't everyone as loving as we? Did you see our cute, wriggling, swimming babies? Who wouldn't want to hold one, cuddle one, breast feed one?... Strange, selfish creatures the humans. We love your babies so much... Do you know how many of us share your DNA? This world could be beautiful... *liberté, egalité, fraternité* as my linguist sister would have said in Chinese. What's French?

Oh, thank you, I remind you of the French...

*

the gourmet

...adding a few selected polypeptides (family secret), a touch of hemagglutinins, maybe some prostaglandins especially for type A blood in the afternoon... *miam-miam*, is there anything better in this world? No, not even Belgian mayonnaise. Chocolate? What's chocolate?

I like mayonnaise smeared on the fat finger throbbing with blood rich in proteins and sugars of that big voluptuous blonde at number 76 just after her cream-rich cake and cheese dinner... *lekka-lekka*. No, it's not a storm, it's my abdomen, I suddenly got this whiff of 1-octen-3-ol from you... hey, wait, let's share, as my leftist sister would have said... *fucka-(oopsa)-licka-good*!!!

Fifty Love Declarations

She made a horrible face, when I told her that I loved her, her tears swelling. You, women, are not happy even when one loves you as much as I do. Her tears evaporated in the sun of a smile. *You didn't mention 'much' before,* she snuggled against me, cooing.

*

Say it differently, she challenged me. I-don't-don't-love-you, I said. uoy-evol-I on a Semitic typewriter. india-limaoscarvictorecho-yankeeoscaruniform. dididadadadididadadadadididad-dadidadadadadadidida. dw-i'n-dy-garu-di. *What's that, Elvish?* No, that would be le-melon. Welsh. Woof! I continued. One syllable is all a dog would need. *And a tail,* she smiled, looking for the tail but finding the mouth.

*

We walk hand in hand. We walk hand in hand. We walk hand in hand. *How many times do you intend to repeat it?* Until we reach fifty words. I promised you a love declaration in fifty words, didn't I? We walk hand in hand. We walk hand in hand.

Species

species, one

"Mommy, where are your tits?" I asked.

"Crocodiles don't have tits, baby, we are cold blooded blood suckers, not milk suckers," and she gave me a swift demonstration.

"But I want to be vegetarian, mommy."

She rolled her eyes in the universal sign of 'what next?'.

"And I'll be the laughing of the neighborhood."

"Mommy..."

"Yes?"

"Why don't we tell humans that we can talk, then they may get so curious that they will stop hunting us for making boots."

"Oh, poor innocent you. Because humans have one characteristic even stronger than curiosity, baby."

"Which one, mommy?"

"Greed, baby. Greed."

*

species, two

I ran into the shop, my skirt fluttering wildly behind me.

"Papa, papa, come here," I shouted, connecting the camera to the TV. Two crocodiles wagging their tails appeared on the screen.

"*So?*" he asked impatiently. I turned up the sound. He paled, disconnected the camera and placed it gently on the floor, then in one swift move smashed it with his heel. "*We have a business to run,*" he muttered, crossing between racks sagging under the weight of boots and shoes and dropping the shards in the bin. "*I'll buy you a better one, don't worry.*"

I started crying.

*

species, three

"They'll never let us marry," she said, angrily hitting the lake with a pebble.

He lay on his back, watching butterflies fluttering above his belly. They always took his belly for a flower.

"Racists," he bellowed, the butterflies dispersing. She went over and curled herself into his warmth, sliding a hand into her pocket. "I want to see the sunset," he added, touching softly her hair.

Southern Herald

...*a dead teenager girl was found on the South Bank, next to a dead crocodile. Both seem to have been shot through the head. The crime weapon was found nearby. Police investigates...*

end of book Four of the Short Stories collections

I woke up to the word too late. I have a lot of catch-up to do, I will certainly fail.

So what? The fun is in the chase, the traps, the slippery stains of oil and the poisoned arrows buzzing here and there past my ears. Onehundredworders are a blessing, allowing me to a certain extent to dress a bit of flesh around all these many ideas I would, otherwise, never have had the time to finish.

Don't underestimate the effort. The time it takes – yes, much shorter than real stories, even much shorter than short stories. The pleasure, I dare say, much... bigger, more intense, dense, sharp.

After all, each concluded effort is comparable to an orgasm, each finished story a new, eternal lover. Oh, I love my harem.

Yossi Faybish